BROWNIE POINTS FOR MURDER

A JILL ANDREWS COZY MYSTERY

NICOLE ELLIS

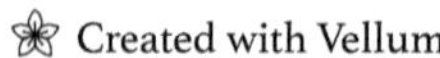
Created with Vellum

1

With the last white linen tablecloth accounted for on my inventory list, I exited the storeroom into the main hallway of the Boathouse Event Center. Outside, waves slapped against the pilings, drawing me to the picture windows overlooking the dock. I'd lived in the Seattle area for over ten years, but the ever-changing scenery of Puget Sound never failed to fascinate me.

Today, the unseasonably warm April weather had lured hundreds of eager boaters to the water. Motorboats churned up waves behind them and sailboats slid like silk through the blue-gray water, sails flapping in the strong spring breeze. Further away, the Willowby Island car ferry chugged toward the Ericksville dock.

One of the few things that could distract me from the view, the aroma of melting chocolate, wafted through the building. I followed the scent to the kitchen, where I found Desi Torres, my sister-in-law and baker extraordinaire, peering into an open oven. She beamed and waved an oven mitt at me before reaching into the oven.

"Jill, you've got to try these. I think I may have created

the world's most perfect dessert." Desi set the hot pan on a wire cooling rack on the kitchen island's gray marbled countertop. She cut a piece off of a previous batch and held the caramel-coated confection out to me.

I eyed the treat and mentally counted the calories I'd consumed earlier in the day. Eh, who was I kidding? There was no way to resist. I bit into the bar cookie and nearly swooned.

"What is it?"

Desi smiled smugly and smoothed a cocoa-smudged apron over her very pregnant belly. "I'm calling it a Caramel Chocolate Caress—perfect for the dessert bar at the wedding reception tomorrow." She took one for herself and refilled her coffee mug from the carafe on the counter. "Want a cup?"

"Sure, why not?" Cutting carbs and caffeine could wait another day. I reached for another cookie before I could stop myself. "Hey, aren't you supposed to be taking it easy?" I asked.

"I am taking it easy." She sat down on a stool. "See? I'm sitting."

I took the coffee cup from her. "Well, let me know if you need help with anything. That's why I'm helping out at the Boathouse, so you don't have to work so hard."

She rolled her eyes at me. "I appreciate your offer, but I'm fine. Oh, and look at this." She grabbed a pipette filled with blue icing and deftly drew a heart on top of one of the cooled cookie bars. Not for the first time, I found myself envying her talents in the kitchen.

"Your mom's going to love them." My mother-in-law, Beth, oversaw the majority of the event planning at the Boathouse and took great pride in the details.

"I hope so. Normally, big weddings don't faze Mom, but

this bride is stressing her out." She took a bite of the frosted cookie bar. "Yum. I think I'll serve these at the café too. I'm planning a three-year anniversary celebration for the Beans-Talk Café. Our customers will go crazy for these."

"You're lucky to have the BeansTalk. Sometimes I feel like the only people I ever see are under four." I sat on a metal stool facing Desi.

"Adam's still traveling a lot? Are things getting better for you guys?" She sipped her coffee and watched my face.

I gulped my coffee instead of responding. Saying that my husband traveled a lot was an understatement. A lawyer for a large Seattle firm, he'd been out of town for much of the last two weeks while working on a big case.

She arched one eyebrow. "I take it he hasn't been around much?"

"He's still out of town more than he's here. I feel like a single parent and I know Mikey misses him." I tapped my feet against the bottom rung of the stool. Our preschool-aged son talked about his dad frequently and didn't understand why he was never home. At this stage, our infant daughter was too young to miss him, but soon her father's absence would affect her too. "I've been thinking about going back to work, but I don't know if this is the right time."

"There's never a right time. Sometimes you just have to go for it and make it the right time. Tomàs and I leapt into opening the café when we saw the Available for Lease sign on the lighthouse keeper's cottage, and we haven't once regretted our decision."

I didn't want to say anything to Desi, but in case things didn't work out between her brother and me, I wanted to have income of my own. Before having kids, I'd had a career of my own and hadn't had to depend on Adam for money. He and I still loved each other, but I'd seen friends go through rough patches in their marriages that eventually ended in divorce. I didn't want that to happen to us. Our marriage hadn't come to that point yet, but as his work travel increased, our relationship had been relegated to the back burner. I knew we needed something to change to get us back on track, but I wasn't sure how to make things better.

I was considering Desi's advice about jumping into the job market when a man burst through the open doorway. Caterpillar eyebrows nested above his furrowed, beet-red face. Most people would describe the wrinkles as laugh lines, but anyone acquainted with Samuel Westen, my neighbor and Desi's landlord, knew laughter to be an improbable cause.

"Mrs. Torres." He strode over to Desi, his wing tip shoes squeaking on the kitchen tiles. "Your café is located in my building. You can't make changes to the exterior without my permission." He marked every sentence with a shake of his brown leather briefcase. I shuffled back a few steps to avoid being hit.

With slow, precise movements, Desi used a paper towel to wipe the chocolate residue off her fingers and the icing pipette.

"Mr. Westen. How nice to see you." Her icy tones belied her calm appearance. "What can I do for you? If this is regarding the BeansTalk Café, I will be happy to make an appointment to see you. As you can see, I'm in the middle of something right now." She motioned to the mixing bowls and overflowing countertops.

"The banana-yellow paint you used on the window shutters and trim at the café is not permissible by your lease." He retrieved a sheaf of papers from the briefcase and searched for a clean space to lay them down. Finding none, he grimaced and placed his briefcase on the ground, as far away as possible from a dusting of spilled flour. Rifling through the documents, he stabbed his pudgy finger at a paragraph in a legal document. "See?" he said. "No leasehold improvements without prior approval from the owner." He puffed out his chest. "And I most certainly did not approve that horrid color."

Desi's placid smile had slipped from her face and she set down the icing pipette. I knew enough about her temper to back away even further from the two of them.

"It's paint. If I need to, I can paint over the yellow with a different color. But I'm not going to paint over it. I think the yellow makes the building more appealing. In fact, in the two days since I had the trim painted, I've received several compliments." She grabbed the lease from him and flipped through it until she found the page she was looking for. "And see?"

She held the lease up so close to his face that he wouldn't need glasses to see the text. Strands of curly auburn hair had escaped her tight bun, and her fair skin flushed with indignation.

Westen leaned back and took the lease from her as she continued speaking.

"It also says, 'landlord will maintain the exterior of the premises.' The exterior of the 'premises' hasn't been power washed by you since I signed the lease three years ago. My husband had to do it last year after the building got so grimy from a late winter storm that you couldn't see the original paint color. The yellow trim improves the appearance of the building." With her hands on her hips, she stared at him, daring him to disagree.

He paused for a moment and then recovered his composure. Returning her stare, he said in a loud definitive voice, "Well, you aren't going to have to worry about that for much longer. I won't be renewing your lease next month. I have a developer interested in the property for condos."

Desi's face blanched and she eased herself onto a kitchen stool, rubbing her belly with one hand.

"But my café has been there for years. You can't do that."

Westen smirked. "Your lease is up. Do you know how much that property is worth? You've been leasing it for a steal all these years. I decided to rent it out while the economy was bad, but I always knew once things got better the developers would start sniffing around. I may even be able to induce a bidding war." Desi slid further back on the stool.

"Can you do that?" I asked. "Isn't the BeansTalk Café building a historical site? It's next to the Ericksville Lighthouse." I looked out the window, past the towering lighthouse, to the lighthouse keeper's cottage. Cheerful yellow shutters bracketed white window boxes planted with red tulips.

"Yeah, you can't tear it down. The Historical Society would have a fit if you tore down the keeper's cottage," Desi said. Although she stared defiantly at Westen and tried to hide it, I saw her wince and hold her stomach tighter.

I took a few steps forward, inserting myself between Westen and Desi. I picked the briefcase off the floor, making sure to drag it through the spilled flour before I shoved it at him. "It's time for you to go. If you'd like to discuss this further, please call Desi later."

He glared at me and then took a parting shot.

"The property isn't designated as a historical site, and I can do with it whatever I want. Well, I can after the town council meeting tonight." Westen snatched up the lease papers and stomped out of the room. As he exited, he pushed past my mother-in-law, who was standing in the doorway.

"Excuse me," Beth called after his retreating form. Shaking her head, she walked toward us. "What was Samuel Westen doing here? I swear, that man thinks he owns everything in this town."

Tears slipped down Desi's face, and she fiddled with the icing pipette on the counter. "That's the problem, he does own half the town—including my café building."

"Desi, please don't cry." Beth reached out to hug her and then stepped back to look at her daughter. "What's wrong?"

"He's not renewing my lease," she said, her voice uncharacteristically flat. "He wants to turn the property into condos."

"Condos? On the lighthouse grounds? I don't think so." Fire glowed in Beth's eyes. "He can't develop that property. It's a significant part of Ericksville's history."

"Well, he seems to think he can sell it to a developer, and he tends to get what he wants," I said. With Westen as my closest neighbor, I'd run up against him a few times myself. "He indicated the town council would be approving the sale at their monthly meeting tonight."

"But he's on the town council. That's a conflict of interest to use his influence to benefit his own business dealings. I'm going to go down there and give them a piece of my mind," said Beth. "The café building is part of our town's heritage, and he's not going to mess with my daughter's business." She wrapped well-toned arms around Desi's shoulders, her eyes burning with determination.

"Mom, you don't have to do that." Desi pulled away, drew herself up to her full height of five feet, two inches and jutted out her chin. "I'm going to go tonight and present my case to the town council. They can't do this. The BeansTalk

Café is a huge part of this community, and they sure as heck aren't going to take that away from me or the town. Even if he gets approval tonight, I'm going to do everything I can to keep the building from being torn down." Her eyes blazed with a flame that rivaled her mother's.

"I'll go with you. Together, we'll put a stop to this." Beth squeezed her daughter's hand. "Now, time to get back to work." She clapped her hands together. "Chop, chop, girls. This wedding isn't going to put itself on."

Beth turned toward me. "Jill, can you do me a favor?"

I nodded. "Sure, what do you need?"

"I need as many peanut butter M&M's as you can get your hands on by noon."

I raised my eyebrows. "Peanut butter M&M's? Why?"

"I'll explain later. Let's just say it's a bride thing."

"Enough said." I'd helped out with a number of weddings at the Boathouse and knew clients often made strange requests. "I'll check out the Target and Walmart in Everton. Are the kids still doing ok?" When I'd left for the kitchen, my son, Mikey, and Desi's son, Anthony, were playing in the cavernous main hall. My infant daughter, Ella, was fast asleep in her grandmother's office.

"They're fine. I think the boys managed to enlist one of the waitstaff to play in their game of broomball, and Ella is still sleeping," Beth said. She unclipped the baby monitor from her back pocket to look at it, and I heard the faint sounds of my daughter snoring. "I'll be back in my office in a minute."

I turned to Desi. "Thanks for the treats. These are a definite winner. And don't worry, we'll figure something out to stop Westen from developing the property." I gave her a quick hug and swiped another Caramel Chocolate Caress for the road.

On the way out of the Boathouse, I ducked my head into Beth's office and confirmed Ella was still asleep. As I exited, I popped the bar cookie into my mouth. Like the others I'd sampled, the chocolate and caramel melted on my tongue, but after hearing Mr. Westen announce his plans to sell the café building, it didn't taste quite as sweet.

That man certainly knew how to stir up trouble. Desi and her husband had sunk their life savings into the café. To lose it now would devastate them, and I didn't want to know how it would affect Desi's pregnancy.

2

When I arrived back at the Boathouse with the candy, I couldn't help but remember Mr. Westen's threat to Desi. How was it possible for anyone to be so awful? Still deep in thought, I pulled some bags of candy out of the back of my minivan. A soft breeze scented the air with salt and distracted me from my negative thoughts. With the picturesque lighthouse on the other side of the parking lot and the ferry landing behind it, I felt as though I were in the world's most realistic painting. That is, until a crazed man ran past me muttering "azure blue, azure blue," dove into a Jeep, backed up within two inches of my left foot, and careened out of the parking lot.

I screamed and dropped bags full of M&M's on the asphalt. My legs wobbled and almost gave out. Closing my eyes, I rested against the back bumper of my minivan. When I reopened my eyes, Beth stood in front of me.

"Jill, are you ok? I came out to the parking lot just in time to see what happened," she said.

"Yeah, I'm fine." This wasn't the first time my tendency to daydream had put me in danger, and it wouldn't be the last.

I opened the minivan's trunk and jumped to the side as an avalanche of candy spilled onto the ground.

"And you thought your mother was joking when she said sweets could kill you," Beth said, reaching for the fallen candy.

"Who was that maniac?" I grabbed the remaining bags and slammed the liftgate. "He almost creamed me." I fought the urge to tear open one of the bags and cram soothing chocolate down my throat until my pulse returned to a normal rhythm.

"That would be the groom," Beth said with a wry grin on her face. "His bride-to-be has him worked into a frenzy about the need for the perfect shade of blue carnation for his tux tomorrow. She wants it to match the sky for their outdoor ceremony." She nodded at the plastic bags I held. "How many did you get?"

"Forty-seven bags of peanut butter M&M's. I think I cleared out every store within an hour of Ericksville. We're lucky the Everton Target restocked their candy aisle this week after they clearanced out the Easter merchandise," I said. "Why do you need so much?"

"You'll see." Beth held the front door open, and we walked through the lobby to the back of the event center. The handles on the plastic bags dug into my hands, and I shifted the weight of the candy several times before we arrived at Beth's office.

I stopped in the doorway of her office to stare at the state of the workspace. It had been transformed into a candy store. Several crystal bowls held brown and blue peanut butter M&M's. The discarded colors of candy were piled high in a large plastic container.

"What's going on here?"

"The bride let the groom choose the centerpieces, and

he chose M&M's in cut glass bowls. Today the bride had the brilliant idea to use only M&M's in the wedding colors, brown and blue. She also came in with a long list of things for us to do before the reception."

"And the wedding is tomorrow? That's nuts."

"Yeah, well, crazy brides are part of the business. After forty years, I'm used to it." Beth smiled.

"If I had your job, I'd go batty with all the odd requests," I said, munching on a handful of rejected candy from the plastic bowl.

"It's yours if you want it." Beth sorted through mounds of M&M's with gloved hands. "I've had about enough of bridezillas."

"Why didn't they just order blue and brown M&M's from one of those places that customizes candy?" I purposefully ignored her comment about working at the Boathouse. While I loved the Boathouse, the thought of returning to a business career worried me.

"Because the bride wanted peanut butter M&M's. They only customize the regular ones, and it wasn't until today that she ok'd the centerpieces. She wanted her wedding colors, so here we are. I suppose there are worse places to be." Beth winked at me as she dropped a few chocolate morsels into her mouth.

I hoped none of the wedding guests had a life-threatening peanut allergy. Then again, the bride would never allow it.

"I can't work here—I'd gain twenty pounds in a month with all the treats around." I grinned, but it was partially true. I couldn't stop eating the candy. It was as if I'd forgotten the Chocolate Caramel Caresses I'd eaten only a few hours before. There was something addictive about the combination of salty peanut butter and sweet chocolate. As a child, my health nut parents had forbidden sweets, but I'd made up for it in adulthood. Even with all their efforts to convince me otherwise, I'd always suspected carob was not nearly as good as real chocolate. Every time we went to Idaho to visit them, I went through chocolate withdrawal.

"Seriously though, if you're interested, we'd be happy to have you work here. You know I'd love to spend more time with my grandbabies. I'm so glad Adam and Desi live close by—I only get to see Will's and Sarah's kids a few times a year since they both live so far away." Beth smiled at Mikey and Anthony. The two preschoolers were still playing a rousing game of broomball in the main room. Behind her grandmother, Ella babbled away in her Exersaucer. I doubted they'd even noticed I'd been candy shopping for the last few hours.

"I don't know. I don't want to step on Desi's toes. Right now, with everything she has on her plate, she needs help, but I know how much she loves this place. I wouldn't want her to think I was trying to take it away from her." My sister-in-law had worked at the family business all of her life, and I knew how important it was to her. Plus, it was a handy excuse to avoid talking about the possibility of future employment at the Boathouse.

When my husband and his siblings were young, Beth and her husband Lincoln had bought a decrepit old boathouse and remodeled it into a place for locals to gather for parties. Over the years, they'd added on to the original building, and it had become a premier event center in the Seattle area—popular for weddings, special occasions, reunions, and the like.

"Fair enough, but let me know if you change your mind. I'm getting too old to do this every day," Beth said. "Maybe you could discuss it with Desi before you make your decision."

I nodded and put on a pair of plastic gloves to help sort. Soon, we'd emptied the last bag of candy.

"Well, that's it. I think we've found every blue and brown peanut butter M&M this side of Seattle." Beth carried the candy into the kitchen and carefully covered each bowl with plastic wrap before pushing the containers against the back edge of the counter. She held out the large plastic container with the rejected M&M's. "Can you take this in to Desi? She's using the discards in her famous brownies."

"Desi's making brownies too?" I sniffed the air. What I'd thought was the scent of chocolate candy was actually the aroma of baking brownies. And were those blueberry scones I detected as well? I took the bin from Beth into the kitchen, stopping in the doorway.

Desi had been busy. Scones, brownies, chocolate chip cookies, and the Caramel Chocolate Caresses were cooling on wire racks scattered on every flat surface. I set the container of M&M's on a stool, waved hello to Desi over the pop music blaring from the radio, and turned to leave.

"Hey," Desi called out. "Can you give these to Adam when he comes home? I know how much he likes my brownies." She handed me a BeansTalk Café box loaded with M&M-studded brownies. "You can have some, too, but make sure Adam gets at least a few." Desi shook her finger at me.

I grinned. Desi knew me too well.

Back in Beth's office, I picked up my daughter from her

Exersaucer. My mother-in-law sat at her desk, intent on typing data into a spreadsheet.

"Do you need help with anything else today?" I asked.

She swiveled around and motioned for me to sit in the chair opposite her desk. I sat down, bouncing Ella on my knees as Beth spoke.

"I know you're busy with Adam away from home, but do you think you could help me out with something else? I need to finish up some prep for the wedding reception tomorrow night, but I promised a client I'd meet him at his office tomorrow at noon to get some information for his event. I really don't want him to come here while we're in the middle of setup because he wouldn't be seeing the Boathouse at its best. I can watch the kids if you'd like. They're no problem to take care of here. I may even put Mikey to work sweeping." Beth eyed the paper the boys had strewn across the floor to mark the goal lines.

"A client meeting?" I hadn't intended to get more involved with business operations at my in-law's event center. Shopping for party supplies was one thing, but customer contact was another. While I liked my in-laws, I wasn't sure I wanted to get back into the business world. At one time I'd excelled in a marketing career, but that was in my pre-kids life. I'd quit my job after an embarrassing experience while pregnant with Mikey, and the thought of re-entering that occupation made me queasy. "I'm not sure I'm up for meeting a new client." I played with a strand of Ella's hair and avoided direct eye contact with Beth.

Beth swept a few papers into a pile and looked up at me. "Will you help with the new client? Please… it would be a big help to me, and to Desi, of course."

She had me there. I would do anything to alleviate some of my sister-in-law's stress.

"Ok, fine. Wait, is it a wedding?" As a mother of two young children, I knew I could handle a bride's demands or a homicidal groom if I had to, but coordinating a wedding wasn't high on my wish list.

"Nope, this one's a run-of-the-mill class reunion." Beth retrieved a royal blue file folder from her file cabinet. "I have an information form that I need the client to fill out. It's pretty self-explanatory—just go through the list of questions and find out what he needs. If you have any questions, give me a call." She pulled up the client's name and address on her computer and quickly copied it to a sticky note. "Thank you again for doing this for me. It'll save me so much time to not have to leave the Boathouse to meet with him."

It wasn't until I arrived home with the kids that I read the unfamiliar name and address scribbled on the purple-lined Post-it note. Elliott Elkins. 148 Sunset Avenue.

My heart sank. I knew the address from all the publicity surrounding it. The building was the most unpopular construction project in Ericksville—a new seven-story condominium downtown. With the tallest existing building standing three stories high, it towered over the other structures, blocking views and changing the small-town feel of the business district forever. Although public opinion was against the condos, I had to admit some curiosity about seeing them close-up.

3

The area surrounding the condos on Sunset Avenue consisted of older brick buildings, historic homes, and a few newer businesses. The towering condos clashed with the neighboring buildings, but whatever my feelings about them, they had nothing to do with my promise to Beth to interview the client.

I stood outside my van for a moment, psyching myself up to meet the client. What was I worried about? I had done this hundreds of times in the past, for much bigger clients and business deals.

If you had told me five years ago that I'd be spending my days playing with Legos, changing diapers, and having my main interaction with adults be through the preschool PTA as Jill Andrews, Mikey's mom, I would have driven you straight to the loony bin. Back in the day, I'd actually had quite a reputation as a hotshot marketing executive. Now, I'd traded in linen suits and silk blouses from The Limited for yoga pants and tank tops specifically chosen to conceal baby spit-up.

The memory of that fateful last day on the job hit me

again. I'd been in the middle of a client meeting, proudly showing off the marketing plan, when my huge pregnant belly hit the easel holding my presentation. The easel had crashed into the display next to it, and then, cascading in a domino effect, smashed a 3-D representation of the advertising ideas. Mortified, I'd waddled out of there as fast as I could.

But I wasn't pregnant now, and that debacle had happened years ago. It was time to get over it. I hitched my satchel onto my shoulder, jutted my chin out, and picked my way across the unpaved parking lot, avoiding chunks of loose concrete and potholes that would become vast muddy lakes when it rained. Through the construction mess, I saw the appeal of this location. A few blocks away, Puget Sound lapped against pebbled shores, and the upper condo units would have gorgeous water, ferry, and Willowby Island views. Most of the exterior of the building had been finished, although the upper windows weren't in place yet. The condos had been built in a Northwest style, with exposed timber beams on the outside and a nice courtyard area in front. However, the building looked out of place amongst the one-story businesses and early-twentieth-century homes in the area.

The sign over the main doors read 'Elkins Development Group,' and the outside light was on, although barely visible in the sunlight. I looked at my watch. Twelve o'clock on the dot. I steadied myself with another mini pep talk before knocking on the door.

"Come in," a voice boomed from inside. I opened the door and saw a man reclining in a chair with his feet up on a desk.

"Why, hello," he said. He sat up and removed his feet from the desk. "What can I do for you?" The man swiped a hand over gelled black hair and walked over to where I stood just inside the door.

"I'm looking for Elliott Elkins."

"Elliott isn't here right now, but maybe I can help you. I'm Perry Winston—nice to meet you." He held out his hand, and I shook it limply but didn't offer my name. He didn't seem to notice. "Are you interested in one of our condos?" He looked me up and down and said, "I've got the perfect unit for such a beautiful lady. Would you like to see it?"

I backed up as close to the wall as I could. My creep radar pinged frantic warning signals. The guy was probably in his mid-thirties, not much older than me, but he reeked of alcohol at this early hour and his ruddy cheeks hinted it was not an uncommon occurrence. "No, I'm here to see Mr. Elkins on personal business."

"Ah." He smiled knowingly. I didn't correct any presumptions he may have had.

"Well, have a seat." He motioned to a chair on the other side of the room. "If you need anything, I'll be right over here." He flashed me an oily smile and ambled back to his desk, smoothing his crumpled charcoal button-down shirt before lowering himself into the chair again.

I had barely sat down when another man flung open the door and stormed in, not even glancing in my direction. I tried to focus my attention on a painting of a sailboat that bordered on abstract art, but I couldn't help overhearing the conversation happening twenty feet away from me.

"Perry!" the man said. "We've got to talk. These numbers aren't adding up. We can't hold on much longer." He shook a leather-bound notebook in the air to make his point. "Why didn't you tell me before?"

Perry smiled smoothly and addressed the newcomer.

"Elliott, you have a guest. She said it's personal business." He leered over at me.

Elliott recovered quickly but seemed confused as he walked over to me and held out his hand. "I'm sorry, I don't think we've met before. I'm Elliott Elkins." He wore a turquoise polo shirt and khaki slacks, and his skin glowed with the even color that only comes from a tanning bed.

"Hi," I said, extending my hand. "I'm Jill Andrews. I'm from the Boathouse Event Center. You spoke with Beth Andrews about having an event at the Boathouse?"

Recognition dawned on his face.

"Of course. I was expecting to see Beth. Thank you for coming in on a Saturday. Please have a seat." He motioned for me to sit in one of the two leather armchairs facing a rectangular metal desk and turned to Perry. "We need to talk later. Can you go take inventory of the materials that arrived yesterday so we're ready for the construction crew Monday morning?"

Perry nodded and left.

"I'm sorry, is this a bad time? I could come back later."

"No, it's fine. Something came up with another project we have in the works, and I need to talk with Perry about it, but it isn't urgent. Although, I would have preferred to do this at the Boathouse to avoid these types of interruptions."

Just then Perry came back through the door, as though checking to make sure we weren't up to something scandalous. He rummaged through the top drawer of his desk and held up a pair of black-rimmed glasses. "Can't forget these—I can't read the inventory list without them." He stuffed them in his pocket. Elliott rolled his eyes when the door closed behind Perry.

After he left, I looked around the room. The room's tan

Berber carpet was spotless and the small reception area with plush armchairs practically shone.

"I'm sorry Beth couldn't meet with you in her office today, but I'm glad to have the opportunity to see the inside of this building. I've been wondering what it looked like. This is very nice. I have to admit, I wasn't sure what to expect from a building under construction."

"Thank you. It was designed to be the sales space for the condo project and will eventually be the lobby, so we completed it first." Elliott folded his hands on the desk in front of him and smiled at me pleasantly.

"It's a beautiful location." I gazed out the window. It may have been small talk, but the view of the Sound was truly gorgeous and made good conversational fodder as I mentally prepared myself for the meeting. "It sure is getting warm out there. I thought it was going to rain, but the weather seems to be fickle today."

"I'm sorry, where are my manners?" he said. "Would you like a glass of water? Some coffee? Or maybe even a Scotch?" He crossed the room in five long strides and held out a brown glass from a pyramid of them in front of a matching whiskey decanter.

"Some water would be great."

He filled the glass with water from a pitcher and handed it to me. I accepted the proffered glass and drank deeply, more to be polite than from actual thirst.

We sat back down at the desk, and I pulled the file folder out of my leather satchel.

"I just have a few things to review with you, and then we can go over any questions you may have." I took out my ball-point pen and scribbled on a piece of scratch paper to get the ink flowing. Nothing appeared on the page. I'd planned to test the pens I found in my desk drawer, but Mikey had distracted me with a question about a leaf he'd found outside and I'd forgotten to do so. Elliott noticed and handed me an expensive-looking pen out of a case in his desk drawer.

"Thanks." I flashed him a grateful smile. "So, why don't you tell me about your event."

"I'm the alumni association class president for my graduating class from Willowby College. We're looking to have a fifteen-year reunion at the end of the summer."

"My husband is coming up on his fifteen-year college reunion as well. It seems like just yesterday that he graduated." On the walls, I noticed an old football team photo from Ericksville High School. If he was the same age as Adam, they'd probably gone to school together. "In fact, it looks like you may have been in the same high school class as him. Maybe you knew my husband, Adam Andrews?"

Elliott screwed up his face in concentration. "I think I remember him. Tall with sandy-blond hair? The football team, school, and work took up all my time, so I didn't do much socializing in high school."

"Yep, that was him. What a coincidence. I'll have to tell him I met one of his former classmates." I looked back at my file folder and handed him a brochure with the event space details. "What did you have in mind for the reunion? How many people do you think there will be? Depending on attendance, we have several room configurations that are popular for reunions."

"Probably around two hundred people. Willowby College isn't a huge school, but many of the alumni have stayed close by."

"I've heard of Willowby College, but I'm not originally from this area. I take it the college is on Willowby Island?"

"Yes, it's a small college on the island, only about two

thousand students. Mainly liberal arts, with a good finance and business program as well. It may not be an Ivy League, but it was the best thing to ever happen to me. I want this alumni event to be the biggest and greatest reunion Willowby College has ever had. It will be part networking, part fundraiser, and lots of fun." His face lit up as he envisioned the event.

"It sounds like the main room and a few smaller rooms will work best for you." I showed him an example of the round table layout and photos of one of the smaller rooms set up with a buffet and bar. "If you are doing an auction-type event or need it for announcements, you can use the podium and microphone."

"The main room will seat two hundred people? And that's the room overlooking the Sound?" He opened up the brochure I'd given him and rested his finger below the main room's stats.

"Yes," I said. "The main room is the old boathouse building and will easily hold two hundred people. We've had up to two hundred and fifty in there before, no problem."

"Do you have on-site catering, or is there a list to choose from?"

"We have an on-site caterer, so all you have to do is choose your menu and everything will be taken care of for you." I handed him the sample menu, complete with glossy pictures. "Here you go. If there is something you were looking for in particular, just let us know. We want every event at the Boathouse to be perfect for our clients." I'd heard Beth and Desi go over the sales pitch so many times that I could recite it by memory without consulting my cheat sheet.

"This looks great. We're actually going to be announcing

the alumni foundation's scholarship winner at the event, so the podium and sound system will be handy." His eyes sparkled with excitement. Based on his outer persona of sleazy real estate developer, I'd expected his event to be merely a party dedicated to self-promotion, but there was definitely another side to this guy.

"That's fantastic that your group is offering a scholarship to a student in need. I attended my university on a scholarship, and I couldn't have gone there without it." I'd grown up in a middle-class household and my parents weren't able to help much with paying for college, so I'd worked on and off-campus while a student at the University of Washington. Combined with a partial scholarship, I'd been fortunate to graduate with very little debt.

He beamed. "It's an issue near and dear to me. If I hadn't been given a full-ride scholarship to Willowby College, I wouldn't have been able to attend either. My mother and stepfather worked hard to house and feed us, but there wasn't any extra money for education after high school. I'd always figured I'd enter a trade school or go into the army like my birth father, but I was extremely fortunate that Willowby College was endowed with a scholarship fund right as I graduated. I was the first recipient. In fact, I was all set to take the ASVAB when my high school guidance counselor mentioned the possibility of a scholarship to Willowby College."

I followed his gaze to one of two pictures on his desk. The silver frame on one was tilted inward, but I caught a glimpse of a young couple. Elliott noticed my attention.

"Those are my parents, when they were first married." Elliott picked up the picture frame. "My father was killed in a freak accident in army basic training soon afterwards. If I hadn't received that scholarship, I never would have gone to college, gotten a degree, or become a successful businessman."

"Now that you have my whole life history," he said jokingly, "maybe we should get back to business." We hammered out a few more details, and I promised him I'd have Beth send a contract over to him the following week.

I was surprised at how much I enjoyed planning Elliott's event. It felt good to be back in the saddle.

"Thanks," I said, shaking his hand. "Beth will be in touch about your event."

"Oh, you won't be working on it? You had such a good understanding of what I was looking for that I'd really like for you to manage the event." Elliott frowned slightly.

"I'm only filling in for someone who is out on leave. Beth handles most of the event planning."

"Do you usually work in another capacity at the Boathouse?"

"No, this is temporary. I used to be in marketing, but I left the industry after my kids were born. To tell you the truth though, I had fun working on the plans for your event. I hadn't realized how much I missed this type of thing."

He regarded me thoughtfully. "You know, I may have a job for you."

"Really?" I looked around. "Doing what?"

"I need someone to put together a brochure to advertise the building and then stay on as a marketing assistant. I think you'd be perfect for it. You're organized, experienced, and familiar with the area. It would only be about four to five hours a week, so it might work for you to dip your toes back in the marketing pool. What do you think?"

"I haven't done anything like this recently." His offer was flattering, but when I considered it, my stomach flip-flopped uncomfortably.

"Really, the most important thing for me is that you're a local. We've been getting some bad publicity on this project, and I need someone who knows the community to help us combat that perception. With the retail units on the first floor, this is going to be a boon to the downtown economy and exactly what Ericksville needs to bring it into the twenty-first century." His passion for the project shone through in his voice, and I couldn't help but be swayed.

I thought about it for a moment. I knew Beth would jump at the chance to watch the kids more often. But I wasn't sure how I felt about working for the condo construction project. I didn't like the precedent they set for downtown, but change was going to happen whether I liked it or not and he was right—this would be a good way to find out if I wanted to go back to work in marketing. It was only a few hours a week, so what could possibly be the harm in trying it out? If I hated it, I could always quit.

"It sounds like a great opportunity," I said finally. "When would you like me to start?"

"Great! I think you'd be an asset to our team. How about if you come in a week from Monday?" He checked his Outlook calendar and made a note on it.

"Sounds good." I stood and shook his hand again. "And we look forward to working with you on your class reunion at the Boathouse."

On the way out, I saw Perry stride purposefully across the construction site, consulting a clipboard as he walked toward a pile of lumber. The black glasses I'd surmised were only a ploy to check in on his partner's "personal business" rested on his nose. Maybe Elliott wasn't the only person I'd been wrong about.

When I got to my minivan, my lips broke out in a huge smile. I had a job offer. It might not have been my dream job or place to work, but it was related to my previous career and could be a good stepping-stone to future jobs if that was what I wanted. For the rest of the day, I walked on air. I still didn't know what I wanted my identity to be, but I was moving in the right direction.

4

The rest of the weekend crawled by, with Adam once again out of town. Monday morning found me performing one of my least favorite mom duties—gravedigger. Unfortunately, I knew where a lot of bodies were buried. Corky had been laid to rest almost a year ago, and Artie had passed away close to two years ago. Louie was the latest victim.

"Mom, do fish go to heaven?" Mikey asked, tears falling out of eyes exactly the same cobalt-blue shade as mine.

"Oh, buddy, I'm sure they do." I wrapped my arms around his small body. Water seeped through the worn knees of my jeans from the boggy ground surrounding the gravesite. Somehow, every fish seemed to die in the spring, right after an all-too-frequent Washington rain shower. Adam had better be home for funeral duty the next time.

Together, we piled rocks on top of Louie's final resting place. The azalea bush in the northwest corner of our yard served as a pet cemetery and now shaded three little groups of dirt-encrusted stones, a solemn reminder that life was fleeting.

The distinctive scent of recent rain filled my nostrils. A misting of morning dew covered the grass and soaked my sneakers. Everything in the Pacific Northwest was wet. April showers brought not only May flowers, but even more rainstorms. I should be used to it from growing up in Coeur d'Alene, Idaho, but it was less than two months until June and I could hardly wait for the sun to come out. I assessed Mikey's clothing with a keen eye. He still appeared presentable enough for school.

I stood up, wiped muddy fingers on my jeans, and pulled the phone out of my sweatshirt pocket to check the time. A quarter to nine already? If Mikey were tardy again, the Queen Bees of the Busy Bees Preschool PTA would be after me again. Heaven forbid their three- and four-year-olds be distracted by a child coming in five minutes late. Last time we'd arrived past starting time, I'd received a lecture on getting my child to school earlier. Today though, I needed to keep to a tight schedule as I'd made an appointment for Ella's six-month well-baby exam directly after preschool drop-off. Her pediatrician operated on a tight schedule, and if we were more than ten minutes late, we'd forfeit her appointment time.

We'd found Louie belly up in the fish tank this morning, and there was no convincing Mikey the funeral could wait until after school. A toilet bowl burial with a quick 'out to sea' flush was completely out of the question. No matter how hard I tried to plan our mornings, something always happened to make us late for school.

"C'mon, Mikey, go inside and grab your stuff," I said, pushing Ella in her stroller over to the unlocked kitchen door. I contemplated changing out of my dirt-stained jeans, but there wasn't time. He trudged over to the door and stopped.

"Do I have to go to school today?"

I shot him a 'Mama means business' look. He made a face and ran inside the house.

As I waited outside, I relished the brief moment of quiet in a sea of chaos; only the chirping birds and the far off whine of a lawnmower broke the silence. My yellow rose bush next to the driveway sported fresh buds, and the purple pansies Mikey and I had planted last weekend hadn't yet become food for the local slug population. Down the hill, the Willowby Island ferry maneuvered toward the dock, full of cars and passengers commuting to the mainland. I broke out of my reverie. While refreshing, the quiet had lasted too long. What was my son doing?

"Mikey, where are you?" I called into the house.

"I'm getting my backpack," he replied.

I reached for my keys so I'd be ready to lock the door as soon as Mikey came out. When the door opened, sixty-plus pounds of energetic fur tried to bowl me over. Ella giggled and made a grab for the dog's tail as he shot past her into our yard.

Mikey appeared at the door and peeked outside.

"Mommy, Goldie got out."

"Thank you, Captain Obvious."

"Huh?"

"Never mind, help me grab Goldie before he gets out in the street." There would be hell to pay if our closest neighbor, Samuel Westen, saw the dog before I could get him back in the house. The thought crossed my mind to let Goldie run rampant in his pristine backyard to retaliate for his treatment of Desi, but I nixed it quickly. I knew Desi planned to circulate over the weekend her petition for making the lighthouse keeper's cottage a historical site. Any altercation with him now would make the situation worse.

We ran after the now-muddy dog. The golden retriever saw us chasing him and gave two short barks before jogging off around the side of the house. Luckily for me and the ticking clock, Goldie never seemed to remember which side of the yard was fenced.

I nabbed him by the collar as he neared the fence line and brought him inside along with the kids, quickly cleaning him off as well as I could with a dish towel. Our long-haired tabby cat, Fluffy, saw us. She alternated between eyeing her food bowl and meowing loudly in our direction. When she realized we were drying Goldie off, she ran off for the furthest corner of our house lest we planned to bathe her too.

Mikey had given our pets their unoriginal names. I would forever be grateful that Adam and I had chosen Ella's name, rather than allowing Mikey to name her, or we would have been stuck with a daughter named Baby Sister.

The Disney calendar on the kitchen wall caught my eye. Blue x's indicating Adam's out-of-town trips clouded the corner of almost every square. What I wouldn't give for him to be home more often or—dare I hope for it—a week-long couple's trip to the Caribbean. My eyes lingered on the small calendar of June at the bottom of April's page. We'd gone to Jamaica on our honeymoon and often talked about going back. The law firm where Adam worked owed him some vacation days, and we could definitely use a vacation without kids. I closed my eyes for a second and imagined the warm tropical sun kissing my skin.

"Mom! I'm ready. Let's go," Mikey said. Reluctantly, I traveled mentally back to the soggy Pacific Northwest.

I herded the kids out of the house, firmly closing and locking the door as we left.

My phone beeped once to notify me of a new voicemail.

The call log revealed my former colleague, Gena, had called while we were wrestling with the dog. Last week, in a moment of optimistic bravado, I'd put out feelers about going back to work. I hoped that was the reason she'd called. It would put me another minute behind schedule, but I couldn't wait to check the message. Of course, the moment I hit play, an aging car badly in need of a muffler replacement—the only car I'd seen all morning—drove past, and I had to replay the voicemail twice before deciphering what Gena had said.

"Hey, Jill, it's Gena. I think I may have a lead on a job you'd be perfect for. Call me back as soon as you can. I've got a volu-mandatory work social tonight, but I should be home by nine if we don't connect before then."

A thrill shot through me, followed by a sense of unease. Was I ready to go back to the workforce full-time? The part-time job with Elkins Development Group was one thing, but a full-time job with travel was quite another. I wished I'd answered the phone when she called.

Growing up, both of my parents had been teachers; my mother taught middle school social studies and my father taught elementary P.E. I'd loved having both of them home during summer and school vacations, and we'd spent a lot of time together as a family. We'd camped all over the West in the summers and gone sledding over Christmas break, all memories I cherished. I didn't think I'd be able to create anything close to that for my kids if Adam and I both had demanding jobs. However, I did miss working outside the home and interacting with adults on a daily basis.

My phone's calendar alarm rang, and I pulled myself away from thoughts of future career plans. We had twenty minutes to make it to Mikey's school before he'd officially be tardy.

I pushed Ella in the stroller, and Mikey plodded along beside us in the Spiderman rain boots he'd insisted on wearing. We made our way down the hill toward the preschool, walking so slowly I feared inchworms would beat us there. Through past experience, I'd found it quicker to walk the six blocks to downtown Ericksville than to wrangle the kids into their car seats and then search for parking near the preschool. Today, driving may have been the better choice.

"I want to push," Mikey said, inserting himself between me and the stroller.

"Ok, but be careful of your sister." I hovered over him, ready to grab the handles if necessary. Arguing would only put us further behind.

The front wheel hit a crack in the concrete and rolled over the edge of the sidewalk and into the neat line of rocks bordering Mr. Westen's prize flower garden.

Of course, he was standing in his driveway at the time and poked his head out from the back tailgate of the Jeep Wagoneer he'd probably purchased new in 1980. Pollen didn't dare sully his car, even though he habitually parked the vehicle under a maple tree in his gravel driveway. The rear of the vehicle was crammed full of intricately stacked camping paraphernalia, like a giant game of Jenga.

"Hey, watch it, kid!" Mr. Westen walked toward us, his gait surer than I'd expect for a man in his late seventies. I knew he was deceptively strong because I'd seen him lug concrete pavers around last summer for a construction project behind his house.

Mikey shrank back instinctively and pressed himself against my leg. I put my hand on his head.

"It's ok," I whispered. I stroked his head and made a mental reminder to get him in to the barber soon.

"Sorry about that," I said. "He only hit the rock, and he'll be more careful next time." I smiled and hoped feminine charm would work on him. Adam and I wanted to install a fence across the back of our property so we could let Goldie out to play in the yard, but city laws required a neighbor's permission to install such a fence on common borders. Mr. Westen had refused our request, saying a chain-link fence was an eyesore, even though his view of it would be blocked by a row of junipers we'd planted for privacy. In hopes that his opinion would soften, we planned to petition him and the city in a few months with a proposal for a different type of fence. I didn't want to anger him before we even had a chance to ask. Beth had told me yesterday how he had pushed his agenda to sell the BeansTalk building through the town council, and after hearing that I wasn't positive about our chances to get the fence approved.

My smile had no effect on him. He looked like the proverbial old man about to shake his fist at the young neighborhood whippersnappers.

"Keep your kids and dog out of my yard." He gestured to our lawn, which was visible through the trees at the top of his sloping property. "Don't think I didn't see that dog running loose up there. I'm leaving for a week-long fishing trip and if I come back and find my flowers dug up or dog crap in the yard, I'm calling the cops on you." He turned back to his vehicle and roughly shoved a fishing pole on top of a red Coleman cooler while muttering something about leash laws.

"Old coot," I whispered under my breath as I pulled Ella's stroller out of the dirt. He turned and cocked his head in our direction as though he'd heard me. I avoided making eye contact with him. He may have been a cranky old man, but he could still instill fear.

"Let's go, Mikey." I nudged my son, and we quickened our pace until we were well away from Mr. Westen's house. I had no idea how he'd seen Goldie loose in the yard for the brief period of time the dog had escaped. It wasn't like we let Goldie roam free on a regular basis. My childhood dog had been hit by a car, so I was fanatical about always having Goldie leashed when outside. With all of his concerns about the dog getting into his flower beds, you'd think he would be more amenable to a fence between our properties, but his opposition to the fence was purely spiteful. I prayed I wouldn't be that crabby when I grew old.

"Mommy?" Mikey said.

"What, honey?" I asked, my attention focused on crossing the next side street and navigating up the curb ramp.

"Is Daddy going to be home tonight to read me Dr. Seuss? Or not?" He stopped walking and looked up at me, his expression so solemn I thought he was going to cry. His full-size Mickey Mouse backpack dwarfed him.

"Um, maybe." I wasn't sure how to answer his question as I didn't know myself.

A siren wailed close by and two fire trucks barreled down the main road a block away, heading toward a plume of smoke wafting out of a building near the waterfront.

"Cool, sirens!" Mikey took off, and I jogged with the stroller to catch up to where he stood at the street corner looking down the hill.

"Do you see it, Mommy?"

I did see it. Unfortunately, what I saw was my job offer going up in smoke. The fire was at 148 Sunset Avenue. The bells at the Lutheran church rang the nine o'clock hour, and I reluctantly pulled my gaze away from the construction zone.

"Let's go." I wheeled the stroller around and firmly maneuvered Mikey in the direction of his school. Between the altercation with Mr. Westen and the distraction of the condo fire, we arrived at the Busy Bees cooperative preschool three minutes late. When I saw Nancy Davenport was the parent volunteer for the day, I almost turned around.

All of the children were gathered on the ABC rug as she read them a story. When we entered the room, Nancy stopped reading and looked at my soiled jeans with disdain. She made a point to glance at her wristwatch before pasting a fake smile on her face and calling to Mikey to join the story circle. He threw his backpack in his cubby and ran eagerly over to the group, the lights on his shoes flashing with every step.

5

After dropping Mikey off, I wanted to get a closer look at the fire. When I joined the group watching from the opposite side of the street, flames were shooting out of the rear of the condo building. Community complaints had plagued the project, and I wondered if someone had deliberately set the fire. Firefighters sprayed water at the fire, fighting to gain control of the situation.

I felt the urge to pinch myself to wake up from what seemed to be a bad dream. The condos weren't even finished yet. Would they rebuild after the fire? Was this the end of my job offer? Across the street, a Snowton County van drove up and parked in front of the fire engines. A woman and man wearing all black stepped out of the van. When they walked over to the fire chief, I made out the words 'Coroner's Office' printed across their backs. I sucked in my breath.

Had someone died in the fire? Where was Elliott? I scanned the crowd but didn't see him. My morning coffee turned to acid in my stomach.

Oh please, please let it not be Elliott. I still didn't see

him. The condo building may not have been popular, but if the fire had been started on purpose, I couldn't imagine the arsonist had meant to kill anyone. A restored muscle car roared up to the construction site and parked haphazardly behind the fire trucks.

To my relief, Elliott jumped out of the car. He ran to the building, where a fireman held him back from entering what had been the entrance to the condo sales office. Heartache was etched across his face as he spoke to the fire chief. For me, the condo project had been a means of testing out a return to working outside the home. For him, the fire represented the devastation of a dream.

On the drive home after Ella had been pronounced a healthy baby, I devised a brilliant plan to bring Mr. Westen some kind of baked good to take on his fishing trip. A treat would serve as a peace offering for Mikey's transgression that morning and create favor for us with the fence issue.

Judging by Ella's crankiness, I didn't have much time before she'd need to be fed. I could make cupcakes, but they would take too long to cool and ice. Was there any brownie mix in our pantry? I seemed to recall seeing an old container of frosting in the cupboard.

No, wait, even better. I remembered the brownies Desi had given me for Adam, who hadn't been home yet to eat them.

I glanced in the mirror and saw Ella had fallen back asleep, snoring softly with her head on her chest. I parked in the garage and ran into the house to get the box of brownies from the kitchen. The box sat in the middle of the granite counter with the lid open, displaying a luscious-looking confection of fudge icing and gooey rich brownies studded with M&M's. Desi's brownies were famous in our family and extremely popular among customers of her café. They would be perfect to give to Mr. Westen. What man could resist such a treat? And there was always the chance they'd even help soften him enough to rethink his decision to sell the BeansTalk property.

I slid a small cookie sheet under the white paper box for stability and gingerly carried the tray out to the car. I drove the short distance down the hill to Mr. Westen's house.

Good, the car full of fishing gear was still in the driveway. I parked behind him, cracked the window for Ella, and removed the cookie sheet with the brownies from the passenger seat. The cookie sheet was tacky, but I didn't trust the box not to break under the weight of Desi's legendary brownies.

I carried my offering up the front steps of his house, past a row of red and yellow tulips that appeared to have been planted with a straight-edge ruler, and rang the doorbell. The stone house loomed above me. Massive curtained windows bracketed the door. While I waited, I took in the view behind me. Although we had a nice water view, his house sat on the hill below our house and boasted a gorgeous, unobstructed view of Puget Sound. I could even see the lighthouse blinking over at No Rocks Point across the water.

Footsteps from within the house came closer, and Mr. Westen yanked open the heavy, ornately carved door. He was dressed for the outdoors, in a long-sleeve green- and red-plaid flannel shirt stretched tightly over a small belly and tucked into khaki work pants.

"Oh, it's you." He frowned at me through his heavy tortoiseshell-rimmed spectacles. "What do you want?"

I forced myself to smile and held out the cookie sheet. "I brought these for your trip. They'll go great with all the fish you'll catch. I also wanted to apologize for my son running the stroller off the sidewalk and into your garden."

"Humph," he said. He eyed the brownies and appeared to be trying to decide whether to throw them at me or take them back into his lair. As I'd hoped, no man could resist Desi's brownies. He slid the box off of the cookie sheet, the bottom bowing ominously, and retreated into his house, shutting the door in my face.

I stood there for a moment with my mouth open and the cookie sheet still raised in offering. Did he really just slam the door on me, without even so much as a

'thank you'? He was even more of a jerk than I'd thought.

Fuming as I walked back to the van, I forced myself to stay calm, rather than going back to give him a piece of my mind.

When we got to the school for pickup, Mikey's teacher pulled me aside.

"Jill, I'm concerned about Mikey. He got into a pushing fight with another little boy today."

"What happened? Why was Mikey fighting?"

"I wasn't present when it happened, but another teacher told me he had been bragging to a friend about his dad, the superhero. After Mikey told him his dad was gone all the time fighting crime, the other boy called him a liar and Mikey pushed him off his chair." Her gray hair bobbed around her chin as she completed her rendition. She pursed her glossy pink lips, gazing up at me expectantly.

Sheesh. A superhero? Adam spent most of his time sitting at a desk, researching his current legal case. The kid had quite the imagination.

"Thanks for telling me. I'll talk with him about it tonight." It was hard for me to have Adam travel so much for work, but it must be even worse for Mikey, who wouldn't understand the reason behind his father's frequent absences.

That night, Mikey, Ella, and I ate alone. I tucked Mikey into bed and read to him from the big blue volume of Dr. Seuss stories, but I could tell my rendition wasn't up to par with Adam's storytelling. Something had to give before he concocted more theories about why his dad wasn't home.

It wasn't only Mikey who missed Adam. It had been over a month since I'd had dinner with him, and our last couple's date had been months before Ella's birth. I didn't know how much longer any of us could take his long work hours.

After brushing my teeth, I checked on the kids and found them both sound asleep. I made myself a cup of tea, turned on the television in the living room, and flipped to the local news. They were showing earlier footage of the Ericksville condo fire and declaring it a suspected arson. I leaned toward the TV to see and hear better without waking up the kids. As the reporter droned on and on about the fire damage, I began to severely doubt I'd still have a job at the condo project.

The fire was top of mind, and the first thing I did when Adam got home late that night was to talk to him about it.

"Hey, did you hear about the fire at the new condo project downtown? Mikey and I saw the smoke on our way to preschool." I shivered and walked over to the sink to refill my tea cup from the hot water dispenser. "I can't believe someone died in the fire. What an awful way to die."

"I read about it while on the train. The news said they haven't identified the body, but it's most likely some homeless person who fell asleep in the empty building. They don't seem to have any suspects in the arson yet. Not much of a shock considering how much opposition there was to the construction." Adam filled the Keurig with water and inserted a caffeinated coffee K-Cup. "Sounds like you guys had a pretty packed day today."

"Yeah, well, that's where the excitement ended. The rest of the day was pretty boring." I started to unload the dishwasher and absentmindedly twirled a wooden spoon around my fingers like a baton before placing it in the blue ceramic crock on the counter. With Adam's travel schedule, I hadn't told him yet about Elliott's job offer. "I was thinking about going back to work. I need some adult interaction other than the overbearing moms at Mikey's school."

"What were you thinking of? Going back to your old job? Or something part-time?"

"I don't know yet. I put out some feelers with friends, but I haven't made any decisions yet." Shoot, I'd been so wrapped up in getting the kids to bed that I'd forgotten to call Gena back. It was too late to call her now. I'd have to try to get ahold of her tomorrow. "Actually, speaking of the condo fire, the builder asked me to work on some marketing materials for them."

Adam spun around on his bar stool to face me. "What? You're going to work for the guy who is singlehandedly ruining Ericksville? You know that building will destroy the downtown."

I knew the condos weren't popular, but his response stunned me. "He's a nice guy, and he has plans for community use of the ground floor of the building. He truly wants to improve the downtown area," I said. "It would be part-time, so I'd still have time with the kids. Adam, I need something more. I need to have something that is for me and not for everyone else."

"It's your choice." Adam sighed. "But I would worry about your safety there with the arsonist on the loose."

"Eventually I'm going to go back to work. And I have a job offer now." Well, I hoped I still had a job offer after the fire. I wanted the decision to return to work to be on my terms, not a unilateral decision made by Adam. His vehement opposition to the condo building did make me wonder if I'd made the right decision to support the construction project.

"Do you think this is the right time? I mean, Mikey's already getting upset about not having me around. If you're not here, it will be ten times worse. And I thought you were going to help out at the Boathouse," Adam said.

"When will be the right time? I was supposed to take a three-month maternity leave after having Mikey, and that didn't happen, and then we had Ella." I drank deeply from my now cool mug of chamomile tea to calm myself. "Look, I don't even know if I want to go back to work full-time right now, I just want to know what options are available."

"Okay, that sounds fair. But can you wait a few more weeks until things settle down at my job? We can revisit this then."

Wah! Wah! Ella's cries blared through the baby monitor on the end table.

"I'll get her and then I have to work some more before bed." Adam grabbed his cup of coffee and headed upstairs toward our daughter's room. At the foot of the stairs, he turned to me and said, "Honey, don't worry about the job situation—yours or mine. Everything will work out, it always does."

I wasn't so sure he was right. Tonight's conversation had gone the same route as others, with Adam promising to find time to discuss the issue sometime in the nebulous future. I wasn't able to get a feel for whether he wanted me to go back to work or not, which added to my own confusion and indecision about being a stay-at-home mom. I finished unloading the dishwasher and turned out the lights before going upstairs myself.

Ella's cries woke me up from a fretful sleep. I rolled over to see the alarm clock. Two o'clock in the morning. Tomorrow I would be a sleep-deprived zombie. Adam snored softly next to me. I got out of bed, threw on my robe and slippers, and retrieved Ella from her crib before she woke him or Mikey up.

While waiting for Ella's bottle to heat in a mug of hot water, I rocked her gently against me. Through the kitchen windows, I noticed a light on in Mr. Westen's living room. Someone moved around inside the otherwise dark house. Had he decided not to go on his fishing trip? It wouldn't surprise me if he'd stayed to keep an eye on his yard to save it from being invaded by marauding kids and dogs. Or worse, had he remained in town after hearing about Desi's petition to save the BeansTalk building?

The microwave timer beeped, and I pulled the bottle out of the water, sitting down with Ella in the comfortable brown leather recliner in the living room. I popped out the foot rest and sank into the chair's embrace. She sucked the bottle down and promptly fell asleep. I kissed her crop of silky red hair that matched my own and inhaled the intoxicating scent of baby shampoo, thinking back to her birth. Had it really been six months already? Time went by so fast.

It seemed like yesterday when Adam and I had first seen this house, but I'd been five months pregnant with Mikey at the time. We'd been house hunting for a few months for a good family home, and Adam had wanted to move out of Seattle and back to his hometown of Ericksville, where his parents and sister's family still lived. The Craftsman-inspired house with a partial view of Puget Sound had appealed to both of us immediately, and we'd made an offer on the spot. It wasn't until later that we'd found out the land had once been part of the large Westen estate and came with a crotchety old man for an immediate neighbor. I'd never understood why Mr. Westen had sold the land if he hated having neighbors.

The moon's soft glow on the wall and the hum of the refrigerator had almost lulled me to sleep when a car's engine revved up the hill, waking Ella. In a half-asleep daze, I danced around the living room until she finally fell back to sleep. As I passed through the kitchen on the way to the stairs, I glanced out the window at Mr. Westen's house, but the light was now off.

I lowered Ella into her white wooden crib and turned off the pink dancing ballerina nightlight. She turned in her sleep and made a little cry before sticking her thumb in her mouth. I turned on the soothing ocean sound on her Sleep Sheep in case another car passed by. At night, cars on our side street were rare, but I didn't want to risk her waking up again.

Before I returned to bed, I poked my head into Mikey's room to check on him. He lay curled up in the lower bunk in his room, hugging a stuffed monkey against his chest with a Disney Pixar Cars comforter tucked tightly around his small form. He looked so young and innocent, and I paused for a moment to watch him sleep. When I left his doorway, I made a silent promise to get him to school on time the next day and to find a way to make peace with Nancy Davenport and the other preschool PTA Queen Bees.

6

I woke the kids up early the next morning, but after a preschooler temper tantrum and an emergency baby bath made necessary by a messy diaper, we didn't have much time to spare. Mikey clung to me and begged me to cross to the other side of the street before we passed Mr. Westen's house.

When we came abreast of his house, I didn't see a car parked in the driveway and I assumed he'd left early in the morning for his fishing trip. Miraculously, after speed-walking down the hill, we made it to Mikey's preschool seven minutes early. I was tying Goldie's leash to a bike rack next to the door when Brenda Watkins tapped me on the shoulder.

"Hi, Jill. It seems like it's been so long since I last saw you." One of Brenda's twin three-year-old girls tugged at her well-manicured hand, but she just patted her daughter's head. "I've been so busy with the real estate market turning around this spring, but we should get together for coffee sometime soon."

"Sure, I'd like that. How about after preschool drop-off

sometime next week? We can walk over to the BeansTalk Café together. Wait, let me check my calendar. I think I have preschool helper duty next week." I pulled up the calendar on my phone. "Nope, we're good. That's next month. This week, I'm supposed to be in on Thursday to help with the latest bake sale planning. I missed last month's PTA meeting and somehow got assigned to help. With the tuition we're paying here and the endless fundraisers, I don't see how another bake sale can possibly be needed."

"Ugh, don't you just hate that? I swear stay-at-home moms have nothing better to do than sit around and discuss ways to make other moms' lives miserable," Brenda said. The wind blew a lock of ebony-colored hair into her eyes, and she pushed it firmly back into place behind her ear, which sparkled with a large diamond stud earring.

Stay-at-home moms? Was I being grouped in with the Queen Bees? I suddenly felt queasy and ducked my head down to kiss Ella's head where she snuggled against my chest in her baby carrier.

Brenda noticed my unease and her face reddened. "Uh, you know what I mean. You're so busy with the baby and helping out your in-laws. Some of those moms don't have anything better to do than make craft projects off of Pinterest and get in everyone else's business." She allowed her girls to pull her into the school.

"I'll see you soon," she called over her shoulder.

After we secured Goldie's leash, Mikey, Ella, and I entered the school as well. Mikey ran off to his classroom while I signed him in using the most complicated computer sign-in system known to man.

Nancy Davenport saw me signing Mikey in and jetted over to me, a determined gleam in her eyes.

"Jill," she said. "I'm so glad to have caught up with you.

You always bring Mikey in and rush out of here. I wanted to have a talk with you about parent expectations for the Busy Bees Preschool. You know how important it is for parents to be involved with their children's education. If you could sign up to volunteer for something, that would be great. We especially need parents to volunteer for the All School Spring Clean Up next week."

Shoot. How was I going to get out of this one? A pumpkin-orange colored flyer on the bulletin board above the counter caught my eye. "Fifth Annual Busy Bees Preschool Auction – Auction Committee Members Needed." Another fundraiser? I remembered the promise I'd made to myself last night and smiled sweetly at Nancy.

"Thanks for the reminder. I'd planned on signing up for the auction committee today," I said. Nancy glared at me suspiciously but turned around and entered the nearest classroom.

I grabbed a flower-topped pen from the counter and reluctantly signed my name at the top of the auction committee sign-up sheet. That ought to take care of my good mommy commitment to the preschool for the immediate future. How bad could being on the auction committee really be? Before kids, I'd excelled in my marketing and sales career on a national level. Securing donations and organizing a preschool auction would be a piece of cake in comparison.

~

"You actually think being on the auction committee will be a cakewalk?" Desi's warm brown eyes filled with mirth and her mass of tightly coiled curls shook gently above her bare shoulders.

"Being an auction chair last year was one of the worst experiences of my life. I'd rather go through childbirth again than organize a preschool auction for Nancy Davenport. Then again, I guess I don't really get a choice in that matter." She laughed and lovingly smoothed her blue and green tie-dyed dress over her large belly.

"The auction committee can't be that bad, right?" I eyed the baked goods case on the counter. The BeansTalk Café offered a wide selection of treats, and I was sorely tempted to buy one. I regretted not stealing a brownie out of the box prior to giving them to Mr. Westen. The salted caramels, blueberry muffins, cranberry-orange scones, and chocolate chip cookies seemed to call out my name. My stomach growled noisily. I hadn't had time to do more this morning than down a wake-up cup of coffee.

How had Desi managed to get Anthony to school and be at the store already? I blamed it on having two kids. Who was I kidding? Desi was Wonder Woman. When my new niece or nephew arrived, she would soon have the baby on a proper nap schedule that neatly coincided with busy times at the café.

"I mean, it's a preschool, not a national political fundraiser." My voice weakened as her smirk widened.

"Ha." She laughed again. "Don't say I didn't warn you. Hey, how did my big brother like those brownies I left for him?"

"Oh. About those." I squirmed a little. "He never had an opportunity to eat any of them."

"You ate all the brownies? Did Mikey at least get one?" She smiled at me, her eyebrows raised in mock concern. "You may need to enroll in Chocoholics Anonymous, Jill."

"No, no, I didn't eat all of them. I'm not that bad! I know I ate three at your last barbecue, but I didn't eat a whole box in one day." Ella seemed to have gained twenty pounds since I put the baby carrier on this morning. I shifted my weight from foot to foot and finally leaned against the counter to take some of the pressure off my back.

"Hey, you're talking to a woman who's thirty weeks pregnant. No judgment. So what did happen to the brownies?"

I sighed and stood back up fully. She wasn't going to be pleased about where the brownies had gone. "I gave them to Samuel Westen." I crossed my arms in front of my face in self-defense and stepped back.

Her jaw dropped. "You gave them to that jerk?"

"I had to."

"Ok, this ought to be good. At least it had better be. What a waste of my yummy brownies." She lifted two glass plates off the shelf and placed a brownie on each. "Coffee?" She motioned with the coffee pot at the mishmash of colorful coffee cups in various sizes.

"Yes, please make mine caffeinated." I continued my story, "Anyway, Mikey pushed Ella's stroller into Mr. Westen's flower bed, and he freaked out and had the nerve to yell at Mikey." Every time I told this story, I grew angrier at his treatment of my son.

"Adam and I need to make nice with him because we want him to sign off on a fence between our properties, so I brought over your brownies as a peace offering. He was getting ready to go on a fishing trip, so I thought he'd enjoy them."

"Did he?"

"I don't know. He took them from me and slammed the door in my face."

She snorted and said, "Yep, sounds like the same Samuel Westen we all know and hate."

The café was empty, so we grabbed our morning snack

and walked up the ramp to the back of the room. A half-level up from the rest of the café, the play nook boasted tables overlooking the Ericksville Lighthouse grounds. Outside, on the adjoining deck, Goldie lay with his head on his paws, his eyes following the few people on the beach below.

Desi had constructed a kids play area in the upper area of the café, complete with a train table, toy kitchen, Legos, Barbie doll playhouse, and a treasure chest full of miscellaneous toys. Living in the rainy Pacific Northwest, it was the perfect place to have a cup of coffee while your children played safely indoors. Ella squirmed in her carrier, and I set her down in an Exersaucer. She babbled at us and spun around happily.

"So how did the town council meeting go?" I had heard from Beth that the sale had been approved, but I hadn't had a chance before now to get the details from Desi. I sat down in an overstuffed leather arm chair and dug into my brownie. Yum, chocolate-y goodness. Now I really regretted giving the others to Mr. Westen.

"Not well," Desi said, sipping her coffee. "Turns out Westen has a developer lined up to buy the site for another one of those big condo developments." She set the coffee cup down.

"Can you imagine it? A big condo here, right next to the historic lighthouse? Over the last three years, I've put everything Tomàs and I have into the business. All that time and money. We were on track to make a decent profit this year." Her hands flew rapidly in small gestures with every word as she grew more indignant. "Not that any of it matters now—my lease runs out next month. I went to his house yesterday to see if he'd reconsider, but he wouldn't even talk to me."

Desi winced and held her stomach with both hands.

"What's wrong?" I asked, icy dread churning in my stomach. "Is it the baby?"

"Just a little Braxton Hicks contraction. I've been having them all morning. It'll pass—stop being such a worrywart."

"I'm sorry, I can't help it. I worry about you. With your history, you need to put your legs up and relax, not be on your feet all day. When I come back this afternoon to train on the cash register, I'm going to make you take a break."

"You sound just like Tomàs." Desi removed her hands from her belly to take another sip of coffee. "I made it to thirty-seven weeks with Anthony, and my doctor said everything is going great with this pregnancy—my blood pressure is just fine so far. There's no reason to think it will happen again." Her face darkened, and I could tell she was thinking about the little girl she had lost.

"So what did Mr. Westen say? Will the sale happen immediately, or do you have time to make alternate plans?" I hoped a change of subject would distract her from her thoughts.

"He's in talks with the developer. It looks like I'm going to lose the place at the end of my lease. I can't afford to buy the building—not if I'm competing with a developer."

"Isn't this a historic site?" I looked around. The Beans-Talk building had been built next door to the historic lighthouse in the early 1900s to house the lighthouse keeper and their family. I couldn't imagine it being replaced with modern steel and glass condos looming high over the lighthouse grounds.

"Nope, it hasn't previously been designated as such—that's a perk of being on the town council. Westen's managed to use his position to block the historic designation every time it's come up. And now he's going to cash in. I'm going to create a petition for people to sign to make it a historic preservation site, but who knows if that will work."

"I'm so sorry, Desi. I know how much the BeansTalk means to you. Maybe you could move it to a new location?"

She sighed. "It wouldn't be the same. There aren't any other waterfront locations available and so much of my business comes from the ferry traffic. I'm afraid I'll have to shut down the café. Business has been booming lately, and I had planned to tell my parents soon I'd be leaving my job at the Boathouse to work here full-time. So much for that dream."

Jingle, jingle. The bells on the front door chimed, signifying Desi had a customer.

"I've got to go." She nodded at the customer waiting in front of the espresso counter. "I need every sale I can get." She pushed herself up from the wooden chair, rubbed her back, and trod slowly down the ramp, her hand tracing the wrought-iron railing. I drained my cup, tidied up our dishes, and sat back for a minute in my chair.

Outside, seagulls strutted their stuff on the lighthouse grounds, and waves lapped at the pebbled beach. Inside, artwork for sale by local artists lined the walls of the main café space. In the children's play area, Desi had painted a bright mural of vines and sky, a scene straight out of "Jack and the Beanstalk." Local writing and moms groups met weekly at the BeansTalk and students studied there, fueled by caffeine and sugar. The community needed the café, and its demise would leave a void in the tapestry of small-town life.

My stomach twisted into a series of knots at the thought of a developer getting their hands on this property. Small mom-and-pop businesses like the BeansTalk were part of what made Ericksville a family-friendly and cozy place to live. We needed to support local businesses and not allow a corrupt town council to line their own pockets with money from developers. In the past, I'd harbored a strong dislike for Mr. Westen. Now I wanted to kill him.

Desi was deep in conversation with a woman whose tailored blouse and pencil skirt were a telltale sign she was on a break from her office job. After I cleaned off our table, I waved goodbye and left the café. Before we set off for the beach, Goldie and I stopped off at the Elmer's Sea of Fish walk-up window. I hadn't wanted to disturb Desi while she was with a customer, but I desperately needed a shot of something after hearing about Mr. Westen ruining Desi's livelihood. I would have preferred it to be a shot of tequila, but considering it wasn't even eleven o'clock yet, I settled for a double-shot latte. While I waited, the lunch crowd began to arrive, calling out their fried fish orders at the first window and paying at the next window. A woman who must have been a tourist made the mistake of standing in the pay line before ordering and threw a fit when she was instructed to go stand in the other line first. I tried to hide a smile as I walked past her. I'd made the same mistake the first time Adam had taken me to Elmer's. I sipped my coffee and tried to relax as I walked past the marina to get to the beach entrance.

7

Once there, Goldie tugged at the leash insistently. I held Ella off to the side and swigged the last bit of coffee before throwing the cup in a trash can. The best part of living in Ericksville was the proximity to Puget Sound. The dog lived for the days I let him run on the beach—with an extendable leash of course. A nice long walk with sand under my feet and the sound of waves lapping peacefully at the shore was exactly what I needed to clear my head. Even Ella cooperated by taking her morning nap in her front carrier.

We strolled away from the ferry dock and the beach-goers who had come out in droves on the beautiful spring morning. Goldie pulled me toward a flock of seagulls, his golden ears flapping, and exuberantly scattered the birds. Behind us, the ferry's horn bellowed and the boat chugged away from the dock. The wind had picked up a little, and whitecaps floated on the waves. In the water, sailboats picked up speed, their brightly colored sails fluttering in the wind. A jogger I'd never seen before passed me going the opposite direction and said "Hello" under his breath. I smiled back and returned the greeting as he breezed by. This was small-town living.

Goldie and I continued on down the beach, past the No Trespassing sign at the end of the public beach. Mr. Westen's house sat on the hillside above the beach, and he owned the adjoining land all the way down to the low-tide mark. His car hadn't been in the driveway when we'd walked past this morning, so I assumed he'd left on his fishing trip and wouldn't be around to complain about any trespassers. Gazing up into the trees, I caught a glimpse of our gray-blue Craftsman-style house peeking out from behind his house.

I sat on a log facing the water, and Goldie nosed around at a piece of dried seaweed glued to a piece of driftwood by sand and saltwater. I slipped my shoes and socks off and pushed my feet into the sand. Under a damp top layer, the sand remained dry and sifted gently between my toes. I breathed deeply of the air—salty, with a hint of creosote from the ferry landing pilings. In the distance, children laughed on the playground. As if by magic, the stress and anger I'd experienced earlier melted away.

Sometimes I felt like pieces of the woman I had been before having kids slipped away from me, year by year. I'd given up my career and independence when Mikey was born. But was being "just" Ella and Mikey's mommy such a bad thing?

I glanced down at the still sleeping Ella and was grateful to have had the moments I'd experienced with her and her older brother. Still, it felt like a large part of me was missing.

It wouldn't hurt to find out if there was a place for me in the working world. Desi had her café, and Brenda had her real-estate business. They both managed to balance their home life and work responsibilities. It could be done. But at what cost? And what would the kids' lives be like if both Adam and I had busy careers?

I checked my watch. Almost eleven. If I called now, I might be able to return Gena's call and catch her at work, or leave a message for her to call me back. Before I could chicken out, I clicked on Gena's phone number and hit Send. After three rings, I expected my call to go to voicemail, but to my surprise, Gena's no-nonsense voice came over the line.

"Hello, Gena speaking."

"Hi, Gena, it's Jill Andrews."

"Oh, hi, Jill, I'm so glad you called back." Gena relaxed and her voice bubbled out of the phone. In the background, I heard the sound of a pen tapping rhythmically against her desk and the chatter of muffled voices. "I had cocktails with a friend earlier this week, and she mentioned that Palmer and Diggs is searching for a marketing manager. It sounded right up your alley, so I told her all about you. She's eager to meet you."

"Oh." I was quiet for a moment. "That sounds... great."

"You don't sound as enthusiastic as I'd have thought," Gena said. "Is everything alright?"

"Yes, of course. Sorry. That sounds like a fantastic opportunity. I would love to speak with her to find out if I'm a good fit for the position." It didn't hurt to check things out and I didn't want to burn any bridges with Gena before assessing the job. I rested my hand on Ella's sleeping form and smoothed the covering over her bare head to block the breeze off the water. "Full disclosure, though, I haven't completely decided if I'm ready to go back to work."

"Well, just give her a call to find out and go from there. Now where did I put her phone number?"

I heard rustling and I imagined Gena rummaging

around for a business card in the giant leather suitcase she called a handbag.

Goldie barked sharply three times from behind me and tugged at the leash.

"Cut it out," I whispered loudly to the dog. I pushed myself up from the beach log to avoid having Goldie pull Ella and I backwards.

"What's going on?" Gena asked.

Before I could answer her, Goldie tore the leash out of my hand and galloped across the railroad tracks to the base of the hillside. I struggled to force my feet into my Nikes but gave up and chased barefoot after him. On the far side of the tracks, he nudged at a piece of red and green cloth sticking up over the side of a tree that had fallen off the eroding cliff. At first glance, it looked like a Christmas decoration.

I ran over to him as fast as I could with bare feet and noticed the plaid flannel cloth hung on something. A second glance told me that something was a human arm. And attached to the arm was a very dead body.

"Gena, I've got to go." I hung up the phone before she could answer.

8

I yanked Goldie away by his collar as I blindly retreated backward, not pausing until I had passed the railroad tracks. My heart raced. Was that who I thought it was?

My foot caught on a beach log and I toppled sideways, catching myself with my right hand so I wouldn't land directly on Ella. Goldie's leash slipped out of my hand. Surprised at the abrupt wake-up, Ella wailed loud enough to scare away every seagull in the vicinity. As the birds scattered, Goldie turned his attention to the seagulls and chased after them.

"Goldie," I called. "Get back here!" For once in his life, he listened to me and trotted back with a goofy look on his face, oblivious to the man's body lying twenty feet away from us. Ella continued to cry, and I made soothing noises as I got to my feet and grabbed the dog's leash. Had I been mistaken about what I'd seen?

I re-crossed the railroad tracks and walked over to the base of the eroding cliff side to get a closer look. My earlier impression of the man's identity was correct. Samuel Westen's body lay smashed on the rocky terrain. Absurdly, my first thought was relief that he hadn't seen Goldie off-leash on the beach.

Had he fallen from the path on his property, high above the beach? On the path, a squirrel scampered along the cliff's edge, sending pebbles down the steep incline. A fall from that height would easily cause serious harm or death. The blood and dirt covering the body and the awkward angle of his limbs indicated the scenario was likely. I choked back vomit and backed away to the safety of the beach. As much as I disliked the man, I didn't want him dead.

I pulled the cell phone out of my pocket to call 911. Goldie tugged on the leash, and the phone slipped out of my grasp and fell to the sand. I managed to retrieve the phone after twisting from side to side while clumsily bent over the baby carrier. Just as the call connected, a train came around the bend. I struggled to hear the 911 operator over the train's rumblings, Goldie's barks, and Ella's wails, but managed to communicate my name and a request to have the police come because I'd found a body.

After the train passed, I perched on a beach log a few feet from the body and attempted to shield Ella from the sight. I knew she couldn't understand the situation, but I didn't want it to be the cause of any psychiatric sessions for her later in life.

My eyes locked on his body as though magnetized. He wore the same plaid lumberjack shirt he'd been wearing when I brought him brownies the day before. But why had he decided to take a walk along the cliff instead of leaving on his fishing trip? As I pondered this, a cloud of voices floated down the beach ahead of a rather large posse of people.

When the police arrived, a man wearing a blazer and a

necktie better suited for the boardroom than the beach gingerly picked his way through the sand to where I sat.

"Are you Ms. Affrew?" He peeked at a pocket-sized spiral bound notebook.

"Andrews," I said. "Jill Andrews." I wasn't shocked the 911 operator had misheard my last name with all the noise in the background during my call. Ella gazed wide-eyed at the man while he scribbled on his notepad, presumably correcting my name in his notes.

"I'm Detective Orson with the Ericksville Police."

"Nice to meet you." I wasn't sure of the correct etiquette for this type of situation, as I certainly wasn't happy he'd come into my life or, rather, wasn't happy about the circumstances of meeting him. I laughed. It all seemed surreal.

He looked up sharply.

"I'm sorry, it's been such a crazy day. I just saw him yesterday, packing up for a fishing trip. I can't believe he's dead." I cuddled Ella closer to me. Goldie paced restlessly to the end of his leash and back.

"So you knew the deceased?"

"Yes. He's my neighbor, Samuel Westen." I corrected myself, "He was my neighbor. He lived right up there." I pointed to the top of the cliff. "My house is the blue one behind it—you can see parts of it through the trees."

Detective Orson turned to examine the hillside. Tall evergreen trees lined the cliff's edge, and bushes clung to the roots poking out of the hillside. Erosion had claimed other vegetation and rocks which had tumbled down to the beach below, not far from where technicians were photographing the body.

"A treacherous place to take a walk," he observed.

"Yes. I've only been up there once. There's a narrow path along the edge of the cliff. Not one that I'd like to walk along." Just the thought of being so close to the cliff's edge gave me the jitters. "Another one of our neighbors lost a cat, and a group of us searched the woods on Mr. Westen's property. He was out of town, or he'd probably have had us arrested for trespassing."

The police had cordoned off this section of the beach, but a crowd had formed on the other side of the yellow police tape. I looked longingly past them toward the lighthouse. If only I'd stayed on the public beach. If I could rewrite the day, I wouldn't have come to this part of the beach and, as a result, never would have discovered my neighbor's body.

"Mrs. Andrews," the detective said. He scrutinized my face. "Are you ok?"

"Yes, sorry. This is all so awful." Despite the three doses of coffee I'd consumed, all the energy had drained from my body.

Ella fidgeted and whimpered. I rocked back and forth, but she'd had enough. *Wah! Wah!*

"Is there anything else? Would it be ok if I left now?" I nodded to Ella. "I've got to get home to feed her."

"Let me get your address and then you are free to go. We may be by later today with more questions."

I gave him the pertinent information and turned to leave. An eager-looking woman whom I'd seen talking with some of the uniformed cops broke away from the group and trudged up to me.

"Are you the woman who found the body?" she asked, out of breath from her trek across the loose sand. She straightened the blouse that hung like a flour sack on a body that could stand to ingest fewer brownies and shook sand out of her sandal.

"Yes. Why do you ask?"

"I'm Niely MacDonald from the *Ericksville Times*. I'd like to ask you a few questions about what happened."

"I'm sorry, Ms. MacDonald. I'd love to help you, but I've really got to get my baby home, and this dog is about to tear my arm off." I allowed Goldie to drag me a few feet down the beach. "I already told the police everything—I'm sure you can get what you need from them." I walked away at a brisk pace, leaving the reporter sputtering behind me.

I huffed and puffed my way up the hill to my house, the whole time vowing to cut out the brownies myself. The police had already arrived at Mr. Westen's house. Police cars blocked the sidewalk, and Ella and I had to navigate around them. If he were alive, he'd be furious at the careless treatment of his yard. A few tulips that had once marched proudly in a straight line along the sidewalk now lay on their sides, fallen in the line of duty.

The open garage door revealed his Jeep Wagoneer parked inside. Had he changed his mind about going on the fishing trip? It must have been him I'd seen last night when I'd been up with Ella. Goldie spotted a squirrel in his yard and took off after it, with me attached. Ella screeched, and all the police personnel turned to look at us.

I waved my hand toward the dog, mouthed "Sorry," and pulled Goldie firmly toward me and the sidewalk. As we passed by the open garage, I noticed the vehicle was still loaded with the fishing paraphernalia I'd seen Mr. Westen pack the day before.

While I fed Ella her bottle, I glanced out the window. People were scurrying around in my neighbor's house. It seemed like overkill for an accidental death, but maybe his death received special treatment due to his status as an esteemed town councilman. Ericksville's small police force must have had their hands full between his accident and the fire and arson-related death at the condo project.

9

After Ella finished eating and I'd done a few loads of laundry, her chin drooped and she rubbed at her eyes, so I put her in the fully reclined stroller seat and set off for the BeansTalk Café. Ella fell asleep before we rolled past Mr. Westen's house. The grounds no longer resembled a raging house party but instead appeared forlorn and empty. The police had shut the garage door and turned off all the lights in his house. The house reminded me of the sight of his broken body lying on the beach, crumpled behind a beach log. I shuddered. Falling off a cliff was a horrible way to die. He had been a grumpy old man, but I never would have wished his fate upon him.

I pushed the stroller faster, as though once past his house, I could push away the unwanted memories. The wheels strummed sweetly along the ground, and a breeze carried the scent of salt water up the hill. The day was shaping up to be quite warm. Down by the ferry dock, I entered the BeansTalk Café, causing bells above the door to tinkle, signaling my arrival. I eased the stroller through the door without waking Ella up and situated her stroller against a wall behind the front counter. The room was empty. I half wondered if Desi was out celebrating Mr. Westen's death and then pushed the thought out of my mind. I didn't want to think about what I'd seen anymore.

"Desi? Where are you?"

"Right here," she said, walking out of the door to the back room. "I was unpacking boxes and placing orders on my computer in the office."

"You really should be more careful," I chided. "Someone could come in here and rob you blind."

"That's why I have the chimes," Desi said breezily. "I can hear anyone coming."

"Yeah, well, chimes aren't going to stop a thief."

"And you think I'm somehow going to do that if I'm in the main room?" she asked. "Thieves could take the whole till before I waddled over to them to ask if they needed help." She ruefully regarded her belly.

She scanned the café with bright eyes, proudly assessing her work. "I'll hate to lose this place. We've been here for almost three years, and now Westen wants to sell the property? That bastard's only concern is money—he doesn't care how his actions affect other people." Her face flamed and she gesticulated wildly at the café walls before taking a rag to wipe at a non-existent crumb on the counter.

Wait, she didn't know about Samuel Westen's death? It wasn't often that something big happened in Ericksville and Desi Torres wasn't one of the first to know.

"You haven't heard?"

"Heard what? I've been in the shop all day." She looked up at me, puzzled. "C'mon, spill. What's the latest gossip?"

"Mr. Westen died," I said. Desi stopped wiping the countertop.

"What? How? Did he choke on a wad of money while

counting his stash? Or maybe one of the million other people who hated him got to him?" She saw my horrified expression and sighed. "Ok, ok, I'm horrible. So what really happened?"

"It looked to me like he fell off the path that runs along the cliff on the edge of his property. Goldie and I discovered his body on the beach this morning."

"Oh, sheesh. Now I feel bad. I didn't like the man, but I didn't wish this on him." Desi bent down to restock the supply of brown paper bags she used for the pastries customers took to go. She straightened to a standing position and rubbed the small of her back.

"It's getting hard to bend over like that." Her face brightened. "Hey, I wonder who will inherit Westen's properties? Maybe there's hope for the BeansTalk now."

"Desi!"

"Well, seriously though. Maybe the new owner will be more interested in preserving the commerce and walkability of downtown Ericksville." She poured herself a cup of decaf coffee.

"Or the new owners could be just as motivated by money as him. Did he have any family?"

"Just a daughter. Her name is Anna, I think. She and her son live in Everton. I don't think they got along with him very well." She screwed up her forehead while trying to remember. "That's right, his daughter is maybe ten years older than we are, so I didn't know her in school, but she worked at the Boathouse for a few years while I was in college. She and my mom still volunteer together at the Ericksville Historical Society."

"Well, if she's Mr. Westen's heir, an interest in the Historical Society is a good indication she'll want to preserve the

BeansTalk building. How do you know so much about everyone in town anyway?"

"It's a small town, and my mom hears a lot of gossip from the staff at the Boathouse."

"His poor daughter," I said. "This must be such a shock for her." Again, I flashed on the memory of his broken body. It was a memory I would be happy to forget but would be ingrained in my mind forever. "Can we talk about something else?"

"Oh, Jill, I'm sorry. I was so wrapped up in my own problems that I forgot you've been through quite a shock today." She shoved a mug of hot coffee into my hands and led me to a counter stool.

The comforting warmth radiated from the coffee cup. I perched on the edge of the stool, and a wave of tiredness overcame me. Between taking care of Ella and performing some household chores, I hadn't had time to decompress after coming home from the beach. Still, dwelling on the day's events wasn't helping.

"Actually, speaking of the Boathouse," Desi began. "If the BeansTalk building isn't in danger of being sold, maybe I can go ahead with my plan to quit my job at the Boathouse and devote more time to the café. I've got so many plans. I could hold an art show here, or classes in the evening, even teach people how to bake." She lit up as she described the future possibilities for the space. Then worry clouded her face.

"But I don't know how my dad will react. He and Mom have worked so hard over the years to make the Boathouse a success. I know he dreamed that at least one of us kids would want to take over for him when he retires. And I do love it, but this place is my dream."

"I think your father would want you to follow your

passion and work hard to make the BeansTalk a success, the same way they did with the Boathouse." The truth was, I wasn't sure how my father-in-law would react. His devotion to the family business knew no bounds, but I needed to say something to cheer her up.

"I know. But I'm the only kid who expressed an interest in the Boathouse, and I know he wants me to run it. But I don't want to shoulder that much responsibility or to commit the time needed to operate an events center. Dad knew early on Adam wanted to go into law, and both Will and Sarah live out of state, so it all falls on me." She rubbed a hand against the deep creases that had appeared on her forehead while we talked.

I set the coffee mug down on the birch-wood counter and wrapped my arm around her shoulder. "You don't need to decide everything about your future right now. How about we take it one day at a time? If you find out you can renew your lease on the BeansTalk building, you can think about it some more, ok?"

She gave me a faint smile and wiped the beginnings of tears out of her eyes.

"So, where should we start? Can you show me how to work this fancy computer register?" I turned her toward the cash register and gave her shoulder an affectionate squeeze. "I haven't worked retail since college, and I'd imagine cash registers have changed in the last ten years." I'd promised Desi I would help her run the café during her maternity leave, but I had a lot to learn.

"Yep, it's all computerized now. When I first took over the space, it was a women's clothing store and the register was ancient. I had to calculate change in my head to check it against the register because I didn't trust the register's calculations. I've tried to modernize things over the years."

She proceeded to show me the finer points of modern shop keeping. Several customers came in for an afternoon coffee break, and I practiced my customer service and barista skills on them. Ella slept in her stroller until it was time to pick up Mikey at school. Today hadn't exactly been a run-of-the-mill day for her either. We made plans to continue the training the next day.

"Hey," Desi said, "if Adam won't be home tonight, do you and Mikey want to come over for dinner? We're having spaghetti and meatballs—I know how much my nephew loves spaghetti. And Anthony would love to have his cousin over to play. I haven't been able to get on the floor to play with him as much as I used to and I know he misses it. Maybe Mikey will wear him out so I can get him to bed at a reasonable hour tonight. I never expected night-owl tendencies to show up as early as age four. I swear they must feed him sugar all day at preschool."

"Sugar? At the Busy Bees Preschool? The horror! Nancy Davenport would have any offender shot on sight. Well, unless it was organic candy, then it might pass muster." I smiled for the first time since finding Mr. Westen's body. "Sure, dinner sounds great. I'm not sure when Adam will be home, but he can pop a TV dinner into the microwave if he gets home early tonight. Do you want me to pick up the boys and meet you at your house? I'll stop by the market and grab some salad mix and garlic bread."

"If you could get Anthony, I'll close up the shop and head home to make dinner. Tomàs should be home by six, and we can eat then." She walked over to the Open sign and flipped it to Closed.

~

When the three kids and I arrived at Desi and Tomàs's house, the smell of Italian food greeted us at the door. The boys disappeared to play as soon as they entered the house. I handed Desi the garlic bread, and she stuffed the foil-wrapped loaf in the oven and tossed the salad in a large bowl.

"Anthony! Get back here and wash your hands for dinner," Desi bellowed down the stairs. She turned and addressed me in a much quieter tone. "I swear, that kid is always on the move. I'm surprised we don't have holes in our carpet."

The two boys ran up the stairs and pushed past each other on their way to the bathroom, their laughter floating down the hallway.

"Mikey is the same way. It must be a boy thing. I don't remember ever having that much energy." I sipped from the frosty glass of iced sun tea she had poured for me. She picked up the large blue-striped pitcher and filled a glass for Tomàs as well, condensation dripping off the edge of the pitcher onto the table.

"Or a four-year-old thing. I don't remember ever being that energetic either," Tomàs said, having overheard our conversation as he entered the room. When the kids were out of earshot, we discussed the surprising events of the day. The timer dinged, and he pulled the steaming mound of garlic bread out of the oven and placed it on a trivet in the middle of the dining room table. I inhaled the aromatic scent, my mouth watering.

"That smells so good. I'm starving."

"You're as bad as the kids," Desi teased. She expertly tossed the spaghetti noodles in with the semi-homemade sauce and meatballs she'd cooked.

"Hey, I never had lunch." My stomach grumbled.

"Yeah, I can tell," she said. "Kids! Sit down at the table. Dinner's ready." The thundering herd of elephants returned, and the kids plopped themselves down at the table. I placed Ella in a highchair and gave her some finger foods.

Mikey grabbed for the spaghetti, and I glared at him. He gave me a 'what?' look. "I think Aunt Desi and Uncle Tomàs want to say grace."

"Grace?"

"Shh..." I held my finger up to my mouth. He did this every time he ate at their house. Although neither Mikey's father nor I were religious, I probably needed to start explaining family customs to him.

"Heavenly father—" Tomàs began. The doorbell rang. He shot an inquisitive glance at Desi, who shrugged. He refolded his napkin and laid it on the table before getting up to answer the doorbell. He peered through the peephole and opened the door just enough to slip out and close it behind him.

"What's going on?" I asked.

Desi craned her head around and peeked out the window next to the solid oak front door.

"There's a police car out there. Probably one of Tomàs's co-workers from the station. They stop by here once in awhile when they need to get ahold of him and can't reach him on his cell."

Through the open windows in the living room, we could hear Tomàs and another man talking. They spoke in hushed tones at first and then Tomàs's voice grew louder.

"Arnofsky, you can't be serious. My wife?"

The other man said something, but I couldn't make it out.

Desi and I exchanged worried glances.

"Mommy, what's going on?" Anthony asked. "Why is Daddy outside? I want to eat."

Desi's focus remained on what was going on outside. I reached for Anthony's and Mikey's plates and served them each a helping of spaghetti and meatballs.

"It's ok, boys. Here you go," I said. "Anthony, your dad's talking with someone from work. Go ahead and eat." He obediently stuck his fork in his food but didn't lift any to his mouth.

"How was school? Did Ms. Rachel have you do any art projects today?" I faked a smile and hoped my face wasn't as ashen as it felt. Something was very wrong. "Desi, what is it?" What's going on?" I whispered.

"I don't know." She stood and walked to the door, opening it halfway. A uniformed policeman stood on the Torres's front porch.

"Hello, Mrs. Torres. I was just telling Tomàs I'm going to need to ask you a few questions about the death of Samuel Westen."

"Mrs. Torres? John—I've known you for five years. For goodness sakes, Tomàs and I sat next to you and your wife at the department Christmas party." Desi's voice shook and she gripped the doorframe tightly. "What's going on here? I barely knew Samuel Westen, so I doubt I'd be much help in your investigation."

"Mrs. Torres... Desi. We're investigating the possibility that Mr. Westen's death was not an accident. Perhaps we could talk down at the station?" Officer John Arnofsky asked. "It looks like you have guests over. I'm sorry for any inconvenience to you or your family." He hung his head and averted eye contact with Tomàs.

"No. You're not taking my wife anywhere," Tomàs said, shaking his head. "We were just sitting down for a family dinner. We can both meet you at the station later, but right now we're busy. Besides, what could my wife possibly know about Samuel Westen's death?" He moved so he stood in front of Desi, who now leaned against the door, rubbing her belly.

At the dining room table, Anthony's lower lip quivered and a tear slid down his face.

"Auntie Jill? Who is that?" The spaghetti and meatballs on his plate were congealed and untouched. Next to him, Mikey nibbled on a piece of garlic bread and looked like he also was trying to hold back tears.

"It's ok, sweetie." I leaned over to hug my nephew. "He's a friend of your parents."

"Desi, I don't really have a choice. I need to ask you some questions. Either we do it here or we can go down to the station," said Officer Arnofsky. "With your son here it might be best to talk somewhere else."

"If his death wasn't accidental, was he murdered? Am I a suspect?"

"No, Desi, of course not." Tomàs glared at his co-worker. "Is she?"

The policeman squirmed and stuck his hands in the pockets of his jumpsuit uniform.

"I'm sorry, Tomàs. I can't go over the case details. All I can say is, we need to talk with your wife."

The fan over the table sucked in cold air from outside, chilling me to the bone. What was going on here? How could Desi be involved with Mr. Westen's death? He'd accidentally fallen from the cliff above the beach. I'd found the body myself. This made no sense. I shivered and rubbed my bare arms. I was rising to turn off the fan when Desi cried out in pain.

10

My heart dropped and I froze in place.

"Desi, are you alright?" Fear clouded Tomàs's voice.

She shook her head and slumped against the door, grabbing her stomach and moaning.

"Something's wrong. The baby. I've been having Braxton Hicks contractions all day, but this is different." Her face paled. "Tomàs, I need to get to the hospital right now."

He took action.

"Jill, can you watch Anthony? And call Beth and Lincoln. Let them know we're heading in to the hospital. I'll call you when we know something." He turned toward Officer Arnofsky.

"John, this is going to have to wait. Can you escort us to St. Mary's in Everton?" Officer Arnofsky yanked his car keys out of his pocket and ran to his patrol car. Tomàs helped Desi, her face crumpled in pain, to their car.

Anthony started bawling and ran after them. "Mommy, Mommy."

I caught him before he could follow them out the door and picked him up, holding him tightly against me. "It's ok, honey. Don't worry—your mommy is going to be fine. Your daddy is taking her in to the doctor to check on the baby." He calmed down slightly and pressed his head into my neck. I fished around in my purse and plucked out my cell phone, expertly speed-dialing Adam and Desi's parents with one hand.

Their mother answered after the first ring.

"Hello."

"Beth. It's me, Jill. I'm over at Desi and Tomàs's house with Anthony. We were having dinner and Desi had pains and thought something was wrong with the baby. They left for the hospital a few minutes ago. Tomàs asked for me to call and let you know." I didn't want to worry Beth with any mention of the police visit, so I purposefully left that detail out.

"Did they go to St. Mary's?" Beth asked.

"Yes."

She shouted to her husband that they needed to leave and then partially covered the phone for a moment to fill Lincoln in on Desi's health.

"If she has to spend the night, Anthony can come stay with Grandma and Grandpa," Beth said to me. "Are you going to the hospital?"

"I don't know yet. They just left. I don't want to bring the kids until she's ready for visitors." I settled Anthony down on the couch and paced the length of the living room. "I'm worried though. She looked like she was in a lot of pain, and with her history..."

Beth said, "Ok, we're leaving now. I'll give you a call when we get to the hospital, and we can come get Anthony later or you can meet us at St. Mary's." Through the phone, I heard the sound of car doors slamming and seat belts clasping.

"He can always stay with us if you can't get him tonight, although he'd probably feel more comfortable in his room at your house." One room of Beth and Lincoln's house had been turned into a bedroom for the boys to stay in when they visited, complete with bunk beds and a wooden toy chest.

While waiting for news from the hospital, I situated the boys in front of the TV with a favorite cartoon and cleared the dining table. How had this happened? Desi hadn't even known about Mr. Westen's death until I told her. In what world was a disagreement over a café lease a good motive for murder?

She hadn't been involved with his death any more than I had. I tried to console myself with the thought that countless people had wanted him dead, and the police would have plenty of suspects.

I scrubbed the dinner plates so hard the finish came off one in a small spot. I retired the sponge and sank into the recliner, hugging my knees tightly to my chest. Now it was my turn for tears, which I tried to hide from the boys. Luckily, they were too engrossed in the antics of the cartoon characters to notice me. If anything happened to the baby, Desi and Tomàs would be devastated. I couldn't watch them go through that again.

The call from Tomàs came a little after nine o'clock.

"You can come to the hospital now." His words were flat and weary.

"How is Desi? And the baby?"

"Desi's tired, but the baby..." He paused. I assumed he'd covered the phone with his hand because I heard a muffled discussion with another male in the background and then

Tomàs came back on the line. "Jill, I've got to go, the doctor's here. She's in Room 814."

I called Beth and Lincoln's cell phones, but there was no answer on either line and I feared the worst. I herded the three kids into the van, and we rode in silence to the hospital.

11

I let go of Mikey's hand just long enough to push the elevator button for the eighth floor maternity ward. Anthony tightly clutched my other hand, causing my wedding ring to dig into my finger. Ella poked her head out of the baby carrier for a moment to take in her surroundings.

The walls of the metal elevator shaft closed in on me and my anxiety levels rose with every floor we passed. St. Mary's had undergone a recent remodel featuring soothing shades of blues and greens, but the pervasive hospital odors brought back bad memories of previous visits. It didn't matter how a hospital was decorated, they all smelled the same—a cross between antiseptic and sickness.

When we entered Desi's room, Lincoln came to take Ella from me, and I went to her bedside, across from Beth.

"Hey, how are you doing?" My shoes squeaked on the linoleum flooring as I walked over to her bedside. I squeezed her hand and she limply returned the gesture. She looked like she could use a week's worth of sleep.

"Baby's still in there."

I let out the breath I didn't know I'd been holding.

She rubbed her protruding belly through the starched sheet draped over it. "They gave me something to stop the contractions but want to keep me on hospital bed rest for as long as possible." She frowned. "They're hoping I can make it to thirty-six weeks, but I'll be getting a series of steroid shots for the baby's lungs, just in case. I told them not to worry, I'm not letting Baby Torres out anytime soon." Behind her, monitors beeped every so often and displayed the baby's heart rate. Anthony's eyes were huge and shiny with tears. I put my hands on his shoulders and nudged him toward his mother.

He walked up to Desi hesitantly. "Mommy?"

"I'm ok, honey. Baby's ok too." She leaned over as much as possible to hug her son. He melted into her and sobbed. Tomàs came up behind Anthony and handed him a Kleenex. He, too, put his arm around his son and grabbed Desi's hand. The three of them huddled together for a moment, silently embracing before Anthony pulled away and stood awkwardly by the bedside. After a moment, he joined his cousin on the couch. The two boys leaned against their grandfather and watched the hospital room's TV. Tomàs took a seat next to his wife, still holding her hand.

"The doctor seemed optimistic that the baby will be ok but said absolutely no stress. I'm going to have a talk with the lead on the Westen case and find out what is going on," said Tomàs. He leaned against the back of the padded metal chair and stretched out his long legs.

"What do you mean, the Westen case?" asked Beth. "What's going on? Does this have something to do with Samuel Westen's death?" Her eyes narrowed, and she went into full suspicious mother mode.

Desi glared at Tomàs.

"It's nothing, Mom. Everything is fine. The police just had some questions about Samuel Westen's death."

"But—" Beth started to say.

"Beth, shh." Lincoln chided his wife from his position on the purple-striped fold-out couch, where he sat with Ella and the two boys. "Remember, the doctor said no stress."

Behind him, boat lights shone on the waters of the Everton marina. Beyond that, I could see clear across the Sound to Willowby Island.

A nurse poked her head into the room and surveyed the crowd. "Does anyone want coffee? I can bring a pot of coffee and some mugs in here."

Everyone shook their heads.

"No, I think we're good. Thank you, Linda," Desi said. She relaxed into the mound of pillows behind her.

"Desi, this is more like Club Med than a hospital," I said, hoping to lighten the mood.

"I know. If I'm going to be stuck in a bed for six more weeks, I could do worse than room service and a water view."

I wasn't sure whether six weeks stuck in a hospital bed sounded blissful or incredibly boring. I wouldn't mind a kid-free vacation for a few days, but after that, I'm pretty sure I'd miss the little munchkins.

Desi's face clouded over as her own responsibilities dawned on her. "What am I going to do about Anthony? I don't want to take him out of the Busy Bees Preschool. Tomàs works such long hours, and I don't think I can get Anthony into an after-school program that will work, much less be willing to take him on such short notice. And what about my café? My staff can take care of some of it, but I don't want them opening and closing every day or placing orders." Desi's voice became more agitated with every word, and I could picture the baby flying out of her.

"Don't worry about anything. Lincoln and I will help take care of Anthony and everything at home, and Jill can handle the BeansTalk," Beth said.

"But we just started our training. I haven't finished showing her how to make any of the fancier espresso drinks, or place orders, or anything." Desi tried to sit up in bed. Her husband gently pushed her back on to the pillows.

"Let them handle it. You've got to concentrate on the baby. Everything will be fine. Right, Jill?" Tomàs stared pointedly at me.

"No problem. When Tomàs is at work, I can swing by Beth and Lincoln's place and pick up Anthony for school and bring him back. I'll have the girls at the café teach me how to make all the fancy espresso drinks and everything else. I can bring your laptop to the hospital so you can place any orders and handle administrative tasks from your bed. Don't worry about a thing." I patted Desi's hand. She collapsed into the bed and placed both hands over her stomach.

"Thank you, all." Her voice was quiet and weak. "I think I'd like to get some sleep now."

Anthony gave his mother a good-night kiss, and Lincoln herded the boys outside. "I'm going to take them down to the vending machine for some hot chocolate," he said over his shoulder.

"Desi, honey, I'll come check on you tomorrow. Give me a call if you need anything. We love you," Beth said. I said goodbye to Desi as well and Beth grabbed my hand, dragging me out into the hallway, leaving Tomàs alone in the room with his wife.

When we were a safe distance away from her room, Beth

turned to me and said, “So what is this about an investigation into Samuel Westen’s death? How could Desi possibly be involved?”

“I have no idea. The police came to their house and wanted to question her about his death. It was really odd because even Tomàs didn’t know what was going on,” I said. “I’m the one who found him on the beach this morning. It appeared that he’d fallen off the cliff the day before. I called the police as soon as I found his body, so I’m not sure what they want to ask Desi about.” All around us, monitors beeped and nurses brushed past to check on patients.

We moved against the wall to allow a woman in a bathrobe and slippers to plod past us. She looked like she was about to give birth to twin elephants. With every step, she clutched her stomach and doubled over in pain. I winced sympathetically. It hadn’t been that long since I’d been in this same hospital in labor with Ella. A man walked beside her, murmuring to her with each contraction.

“Desi has a hot temper, but I don’t think she ever had much in-person contact with Samuel Westen outside of the town council meetings. Whatever the police think, we can’t let them question her and endanger her or the baby. They need to figure out what really happened and leave her alone. I swear, Samuel Westen has the capability to cause trouble, even in death.”

I nodded in agreement. “I’ll keep my ears open. He was my neighbor, and maybe I can use some neighborhood contacts to find out more about him and who would want to kill him.” I suspected the list of possible murderers would be longer than Santa’s list of good girls and boys.

That night, after the kids were tucked away in bed, I finally had a chance to talk to my husband in person.

Adam sat on a bar chair, hunched over the kitchen counter, intent on scarfing down his dinner. The rich scent of the recently microwaved jambalaya I had made the day before hung in the air.

"How's Desi?" Adam asked between bites. I'd called him before I left for the hospital and let him know about his sister and the police suspecting her in Mr. Westen's death.

"She and the baby are ok, but they're going to keep her on hospital bed rest. They're hoping she'll make it to at least thirty-six weeks."

"I'll try to get in to see her. I can't imagine my sister stuck in a hospital bed. It must be killing her." He shoveled rice into his mouth and consulted his phone calendar. "Shoot. I'm out of town for the next week. I'll call her from the airport. She always likes to hear about all the odd people I meet there. I wish I could see her in person though."

"Adam, this isn't working," I said, pacing back and forth from the granite kitchen island to the gas stove. "You're never home."

When he'd arrived home fifteen minutes earlier, he had turned on the lamp in the living room, flung his suit jacket over the sofa back, and collapsed his six-foot frame into an armchair. I barely talked him into eating the dinner I'd saved for him. In the past month, he'd probably lost five or six pounds off his already lean frame because he didn't make time to eat.

"You're working yourself ragged, the kids never see you, and we haven't even had a chance to talk in the last few weeks." I reached up and pulled a mug off a shelf and filled it with water. "Is it really worth it?" I dunked a tea bag in the cup and set it in the microwave to heat. Without Adam asking for it, I poured him a glass of Merlot from a bottle under the sink. He took it with a grateful smile.

"Yes. It's only for a few more weeks and then my promotion should come through." Adam sipped his wine.

"That's what you said two weeks ago." The microwave binged, and I removed my tea. Steam rose from the top, and I wrapped my hands around the comforting warmth of the mug.

"I know. Things came up at work and the promotion got moved out a bit. Don't worry, the long hours won't last forever." He ran his fingers through his sandy-brown hair and sighed. "I miss seeing the kids too, honey, but if I want to make partner, I've got to play the game."

"Mikey asked me yesterday if you were going to be home to read him a bedtime story. I hated not knowing the answer. And he's making up stories at school about you being a superhero, away fighting crime," I said. Adam tried to stifle a grin and failed.

"It's not funny, Adam." I wiped the beginnings of tears out of my eyes before Adam could see them. I was turning into an emotional wreck from lack of sleep. Ella needed to start sleeping through the night. Adam's frequent work trips had turned me into a single parent, and I didn't like it. With taking over some of Desi's responsibilities at the Boathouse and now assisting with the café in her absence, I didn't know how I would make it through the next few months.

"I'll make it up to him. Maybe we can go to the park this weekend as a family." He thought about this and amended his statement. "We'll see. I've got work to get done over this weekend first." Adam polished off the rest of the jambalaya and carried the turquoise Ikea plate to the sink to run water over it. "How are things going otherwise?"

"You mean other than the police thinking Desi killed

Mr. Westen? How did they get that idea anyways?" I wound my hair into a messy bun before I pulled cups and plates out of the dishwasher.

Clank! The coffee mug knocked against another glass cup in the cupboard as I slammed it on the shelf.

"Ease up, honey. The cups didn't do anything wrong," Adam said.

I glared at him and paused before sliding another mug onto the shelf between its mates.

"At least we don't have to worry about Sam Westen objecting to our fence anymore," Adam said. I shot him another icy death glare. He held up his hands in mock defense.

In all the commotion over Desi, I'd forgotten to tell him I had discovered Mr. Westen's body on the beach.

"Adam, I found his body. Well, Goldie found it. He was just lying there like a crumpled rag at the foot of the cliff below his property." The horror of the discovery swept over me, and I leaned against the counter.

"Honey, why didn't you tell me sooner?" Adam looked contrite. He came around the kitchen bar and pulled me close, nuzzling the top of my head. I melted into him, grateful for his support. "Are you ok?"

"I'm fine." I sighed, pulling away to see his face. "But I don't know if the beach will ever seem peaceful and relaxing to me in the future." He hugged me again and motioned for me to sit on one of the stools.

"Do you want to talk about it?"

I shook my head. "I don't really want to think about it." I put my hand on his shoulder and looked into his eyes. "We really need to take a vacation somewhere, just you and me without the kids. It's been awhile since it's been just the two of us."

"I know." He sighed. "I'm not enjoying these long hours either, but I'm trying to do what's best for our family."

"But they owe you vacation time, right?"

"Yes." He stood and put his arms around my waist, tipping his head against mine. "I'll see if I can schedule a week or so of vacation in June, ok? Maybe we can go to Jamaica like we've always talked about. I'm sure Mom would be happy to watch the kids. I know me being gone so much has been hard on you, and now you've taken on some of Desi's responsibilities too. I don't know what this family would do without you."

Tears pooled in the corner of my eyes. It was nice to hear that he appreciated everything that I did because sometimes it seemed like every day was a repeat of the day before.

"Desi's my family, and I don't want anything to happen to her or the baby."

"I know. And your commitment to your friends and family is one of the many reasons that I love you." Smiling, he wiped away a tear that had slipped down my face and held his hand out to me. "It's getting late—let's get to bed, ok?"

I nodded and allowed him to lead me upstairs to our bedroom.

12

After dropping Mikey and Anthony off at preschool the next morning, I stopped at the BeansTalk Café to check in on Desi's employee, Mandy. I'd called Mandy, a sophomore at the local community college, the night before and she had jumped at the chance to work more hours for the coming week because she was finishing up her finals and then would be on spring break.

Mandy was handling everything, but she provided me with a list of things that needed to be done at the BeansTalk, including the baking and taking inventory. I made a note to ask Beth if she'd replenish the baked goods. I'd ask Tomàs if he thought Desi was up to ordering supplies via her computer from her hospital room. I wasn't sure how successful I'd be at managing the BeansTalk for the next few weeks, but I was taking it one day at a time. Beth had begged to babysit Ella, so I was kid-free for the day after I brought the baby over to her.

On the drive home from my in-laws, I paused in front of Mr. Westen's house. There were lights on in his living room. Outside, an unfamiliar Ford compact car was parked crookedly in the driveway. The once neat rows of flowers lining the walkway hadn't perked up after being trampled by the Ericksville Police Department. Crime scene tape fluttered uselessly from the front door.

I continued driving up the hill to my house. After I pulled the minivan into the garage, I set off on foot to find out who was at Mr. Westen's house. Had the police come back? Was I going to be living near a perpetual crime scene?

Based on the Ericksville Historical Society bumper sticker on the car in the driveway, my guess was Mr. Westen's daughter had arrived. I hoped she'd be able to shed some light on his enemies. I knocked on the door, flashing back to my experience a few days before when I'd brought the peace offering of brownies to my truly unpleasant neighbor.

I was midway through a knocking rendition of "This Old Man" and vowing to start listening to more adult music, when a middle-aged woman came to the door.

"Hi, I'm Jill. I live next door, well, right up the hill." I turned to point to my house. "I saw the lights on and came to find out if you needed any help."

"Nice to meet you," the woman said. She brushed back a stray lock of graying brown hair that had escaped her loose bun. Her candy cane–striped blouse was heavily starched but starting to rumple where it pulled away from her trousers. "I'm Anna Westen. This was my father's house."

"Oh. I'm so sorry for your loss. I didn't know him well, but he seemed to be a very... uh"—I searched for something nice to say about my neighbor—"dedicated member of this community." I shifted my weight awkwardly from one foot to another.

"Yes, well, that was the only thing he was dedicated to." Anna's face darkened. "I'm sorry, I shouldn't speak ill of the dead. It really was nice of you to stop by." She paused and scrutinized me, as though assessing my physical fitness. I must have passed because she asked, "Hey, do you think you could help me with something?"

"Of course, what do you need?"

"There's a large couch in my father's den, and the police left it blocking the bottom drawer of his metal filing cabinet. I need to get into the filing cabinet to access some paperwork, but I can't move the couch by myself. Normally I'd have my son help, but he's at school and I don't want to wait for him to get home. Would you mind?"

"Sure, no problem." I nodded my head, and Anna ushered me in to the dimly lit entrance hallway. We'd been neighbors of Samuel Westen for four years, and this was the first time I'd been inside his house. The low ceilings and green wallpaper made the large house feel small inside. When my eyes adjusted to the lack of light, I saw antique clocks lining the living-room walls, mixed in with dark oil paintings of ships. A watercolor of the Ericksville Lighthouse hung over the fireplace and provided a surprising splash of color. Other than the mess the police had left behind, the place was immaculate.

"What a beautiful painting of the lighthouse," I said, nodding my chin in its direction.

Anna glanced over at it, did a double take and then walked over to the painting. "I painted this, back in college. I gave it to my father for Christmas one year, but I assumed he'd put it into the attic. I don't remember seeing it on the wall before." She put her hand on the frame and gazed at it with a faraway look in her eyes. "It's been awhile since I've been here, and I've been focused on my father's office."

Anna moved over to the stairs. With one hand on the railing, she said, "His office is up here."

I followed her up the stairs, which were covered in shag

carpet, to a room off a short hallway. A black leather couch adorned with brass tacks sat squarely in front of the old gunmetal-gray file cabinets. The thick green shag carpeting continued up the stairs and into the room, burying the couch legs and making it difficult to slide. Together, we were able to lift the heavy piece of furniture and place it against a wall in the office.

"There, that ought to work," I said, brushing my sweaty hands off on my jeans. "Do you have enough room now to open it?"

She bent over to pull on the drawer, and my attention was drawn to the wall diagonal from the couch. An armchair sat sideways under the window. Curious about which way the window faced, I lifted a curtain and peeked outside. Through the window, I could see most of my backyard. Now I understood how Mr. Westen had spotted Goldie outside. It would have made more sense to have an armchair under the window on the opposite side of the room, which offered a stunning view of the small Ericksville marina and Puget Sound. Apparently spying on us had been a more enticing prospect.

Which reminded me—last summer Mr. Westen had been building something on the side of the house that wasn't visible from the street, but he'd quickly erected a six-foot-tall border of trees to block our view. I peered out the window and saw a beautiful English garden, complete with box hedges, a short gravel path, and a white concrete bridge over a small pond. Even from above, it evoked a sense of peace and order. That man had been full of surprises.

"Come on." She tugged at the file drawer and yanked hard on the handle, managing to pull the drawer out. Her efforts jarred a model ship in a bottle perched on top of the file cabinet. The glass bottle wobbled and threatened to fall.

I leaned over and caught it just in time. Anna, her head buried in the file cabinet, didn't seem to notice.

"Thanks so much—I thought I'd never get into this thing." She rifled through the file folders and selected one. "This should be it." She looked around at the neat stacks of paperwork on almost every surface. "God knows, I've been looking for it long enough."

"What is it?" I wasn't sure if it was rude to ask, but I couldn't help but wonder what Mr. Westen had hidden in the bottom drawer. I craned my neck around to peek at the documents.

"All of his account and life insurance information. Or at least I assume it is. We didn't speak much in the last few years. As he got older, he became more secretive and money-grubbing than ever, if that was even possible."

"Didn't he ever see his grandson?" Family was a big part of my life, and I couldn't imagine not having Beth and Lincoln in my kids' lives. Even my parents, who lived many hours away, tried to see the kids at least twice a year.

"Nope. Not a big loss though. He wasn't very present as a parent when I was young either. There was always another building to invest in, another dollar to chase. My mother was pretty much a single parent to my brother and me," Anna said, smiling sadly.

"Well, at least your brother can help you out with settling the estate. Does he live close by?" I hadn't seen many visitors at Mr. Westen's house, but then again, I didn't have an armchair pulled up to a window facing his front door.

"No. Benton died when he was in high school." She picked up a photo from Mr. Westen's desk of a smiling teenage boy.

"Oh, I'm so sorry. That must have been difficult for your family."

"It was a bad time. Things fell apart even more than they had before, and then my mother got cancer and passed away a few years after Benton died. She never really got over his death."

"Was his death sudden? If you don't mind me asking..."

Anna sighed. "He died in a car crash. The police suspected the driver of drunk driving, but they were never charged with anything. I was only ten, so I don't know much about it, but from what I could tell from listening to Mother and Father talking at night, Benton had gotten in with a bad crowd. He was a little wild, but he always had time for his little sister." Tears formed in her eyes, and she grabbed a Kleenex from a box on the desk to blot them away.

"Sorry, I'm a little emotional with my father's death and everything. I guess I'd always assumed he'd magically soften in old age and want to be a family again. I was naïve to think that life was like a fairy tale." She snorted and glanced ruefully over at the crystal decanter and highball glasses stacked neatly on an end table. "He loved Scotch more than he loved me, and he wasn't even a drunk. He never could pass up a glass of Scotch, but he certainly passed up all the chances I gave him over the years."

"Don't worry about it, you've been through a lot," I said. "Is there anything I can do to help? I mean, I know we just met, but I live next door. If you need any help with getting the house ready to sell or something, I'd be happy to help."

Anna's tears from the memory of her father's absentee parenting struck a painful chord. I hoped Adam's long hours would be over soon, and we could spend more time as a family. I didn't want Mikey to grow up without his father's presence like Anna had done. I knew Adam wasn't anything like Mr. Westen, but then again, I didn't know what Mr. Westen had been like when his kids were young either. No amount of money was worth not seeing your kids grow up.

"That's really nice of you. I might take you up on your offer. Right now though, I'm not even thinking about selling the house. I'm a paralegal for an estate attorney, and he's going to help me get everything pulled together to determine the extent of Father's assets. At present, I need access to my father's accounts so I can pay the bills for the properties he owns. There are so many business and personal accounts; this is going to take forever to figure out." She picked up a pile of papers, held it for a moment, and then dropped it back on the desk.

The ferry's horn blew, signifying it was leaving the dock. The faint sound reminded me to ask about Desi's café building. "How many properties does he own?" If I was going to be nosy, I might as well go all the way.

"A few buildings down by the water, this house, and a couple others in town," Anna said.

"In all this time of being neighbors with your father, I hadn't realized until recently he owned the building my sister-in-law rents down by the ferry for her business, the BeansTalk Café."

"Oh, really?" Anna said absentmindedly, still shuffling through the paperwork.

"Yes. She's been worried about him selling the property. He'd told her he planned to sell the building. I know it's early to ask, but do you know what your thoughts are for the building?"

"I don't have plans to sell anything. I think I've been in that café before—the one right next to the Ericksville Lighthouse, right? It's such a friendly place. Your sister-in-law should be proud of what she's accomplished there. Before she moved in, it was a retail store. I think the café is a better fit for the space."

Anna put the paper down on the desk and stabbed at it with a capped ballpoint pen. "You know, all of this land belonged to my mother's family originally, and Father just sold it off like it was his own. Why, this house was built by my grandfather, and my mother was born here. It would have killed her to know Father had sold the land where your house now stands. And those buildings down by the ferry should be historic landmarks. Let me guess, he wanted to sell them off to some condo developer, right?"

I nodded.

"Of course he did." She was quite wound up and waved her hands through the air emphatically. "Would you like to sit down for a minute?" She gestured to the heavy sofa we'd moved.

I slid a stack of papers to one side of the couch and gingerly perched on the edge of the seat. It felt wrong to be sitting nonchalantly in Mr. Westen's private sanctuary. Anna pulled her sweater wrap close against her body and leaned back in the padded oak swivel desk chair.

"My mother's family, the Olsens, were one of the original settlers in Ericksville. They owned quite a bit of land around here, including the land surrounding the lighthouse. I grew up hearing stories of the early days of Ericksville." She crossed her arms and looked out the window opposite my house, gazing toward the condo project that already marred the pristine view.

"That monstrosity should never have been approved. It ruins the whole feel of downtown Ericksville, and I'm sure people aren't happy about it blocking their views. Probably another thing my father is responsible for. Thank goodness my mother donated the museum property to the Historical Society before she died, or we wouldn't even have that level of preservation. I'm proud of Ericksville, and I want my son and the new generations to know what it was like in the days of the settlers."

Since Anna wasn't close with her father, I wasn't going to get much information out of her about his enemies, but Desi would be thrilled to hear she had no plans to sell the BeansTalk building. I wanted to leave right away to tell her, but I didn't want to be rude.

"I've been to the museum. It's beautiful. Your mother made a wonderful gift to the town," I said. The Ericksville History Museum was tucked away into a cozy white Craftsman on First Street. The exhibits were well-done and depicted the early life of Ericksville as a fishing and summer tourism destination. The colorful tulips bordering the white picket fence evoked the quintessential small-town feel and never failed to bring a smile to my face. "I'm not a native of Ericksville, but my husband's family was among the first settlers as well."

"Oh, really? I'm sure I know them," Anna said while sorting papers into piles on the desk. "Who are they?"

"The Andrews family. They still own the Boathouse Event Center on the water."

"Oh, right, I didn't know you were related to that Andrews family. I worked at the Boathouse awhile ago. Actually, Beth Andrews and I are still in touch. She volunteers at the Historical Society, and we held a fundraising event at the Boathouse last year. She and Lincoln are such good people. We need more businesses like the Boathouse in Ericksville to draw in the tourists without removing the small-town feel that makes it such a wonderful place to live." Anna stopped shuffling papers. She held up a piece of paper, and her expression clouded over. "Wait, isn't the BeansTalk Café property at 321 First Street?"

"I'm not sure, but that sounds about right," I said. "Why?"

Anna moved her finger over a legal-looking document. "Because it seems my father had already started the process to sell the building."

Desi was going to be heartbroken. "Is it final? It would be horrible for that building to be torn down—it's right next to the lighthouse. Tourists don't come here to see condos; they come for the water view."

Anna sighed. "I don't know. I could have done without this. I'll have to have my boss review the paperwork. It doesn't look like anything was finalized, so maybe there is room to wiggle out of the contract. I'm going to do everything in my power to make sure this sale doesn't go through."

13

To avoid thinking about Mr. Westen's murder and Desi's predicament, I threw myself into cleaning house with more enthusiasm than I usually mustered for the task. I'd already done laundry, swept the front walk, and cleaned some grimy fingerprints off our stainless-steel refrigerator. Tackling the inner contents of the fridge was next.

When had I last made roasted veggies and chicken? Judging by the furry quality of the food, it had been awhile since I ventured into the back of the shelves. I reached into the refrigerator with my rubber-gloved hand and pulled out the offending container of leftovers. I carefully avoided smelling the contents as I dumped the remains down the garbage disposal. Yuck. If Beth hadn't volunteered to watch Ella, who knows how much longer it could have festered in there. I was finishing scrubbing out the vegetable drawer when I heard a knock at the door.

I looked through the peephole and saw unruly hair and an eager face. What was that reporter from the beach doing here?

"Hi." I opened the door a crack. Before I could get "No comment" past my lips, words erupted from Niely MacDonald's mouth like hot water out of Old Faithful.

"Mrs. Andrews. Hi, remember me from yesterday? Niely MacDonald from the *Ericksville Times*. I'm so glad I caught you at home. I was hoping to ask you some more questions about the death of Samuel Westen." She took a breath and glanced at her notebook. "Were you close? How long had you known each other? Did you see anything at the beach that seemed suspicious? Have you spoken with any of the Seattle media outlets yet?"

"No comment," I said, before she could start up again. For Desi's sake, it seemed safest to not talk about what had happened. I attempted to shut the door, but Niely's foot shot out to block it from latching. The door slammed into her foot with a loud thump.

"Ow! Wait," she cried.

"I'm sorry," I said automatically and moved the door an inch so she could extract her sneakered foot. "I said no comment." I admit I didn't feel guilty about the small amount of pleasure I derived from her grimace of pain. She leaned over and rubbed at her toes through the shoes.

She stood and asked, "What do you think about the rumors that your sister-in-law was involved?"

Apparently the "No comment" thing only worked in movies.

"Look, anyone who thinks Desi could be involved is an idiot. She wouldn't hurt a fly." I opened the door a little wider and stepped out onto the porch. I removed the dish gloves to dry out my pruny hands.

"What makes the police think it was murder? Or that Desi was involved?" I was pretty sure I wasn't getting much information out of Tomàs about the case, so I might as well use the reporter while she was in front of me.

Niely smiled like a cat who'd caught a mouse. "Wouldn't hurt a fly, huh? Tell that to the pen she threw across the room at the last town council meeting. That thing was lodged so far into the wall, two janitors had to pry it out with a crowbar."

I narrowed my eyes. "What are you talking about?" Although Desi had a temper, I couldn't imagine her throwing a public fit. But she had been worked up after Mr. Westen's visit to the Boathouse's kitchen, and I knew she'd attended the town council meeting.

"At last week's town council meeting, Desi got into a shouting match with Samuel Westen about zoning down on the waterfront and threw a dry erase marker across the room before leaving. It ended up on YouTube. I'm surprised you haven't seen it." She tapped at her phone and held it out to me. "See for yourself."

I had never seen Desi so mad. She was a whirling dervish of riotous curly hair and swirling tie-dyed skirt as she rushed up the center aisle of the room to address the town council. When Mr. Westen gave her an answer she didn't like, she threw a dry erase marker at the wall behind him, narrowly missing his head.

Niely had exaggerated the force of the pen, but she hadn't been far off the mark with the description of the incident. Mr. Westen's expression when Desi threw the pen made my eyes widen. Even Mikey or Anthony would be hard-pressed to top that performance. I sobered. As funny as the video was, the display of anger toward Samuel Westen had rocketed Desi straight to the top of the police's suspect list. I handed the phone back to Niely.

"She was worse even than that Neanderthal developer

guy. Is she always that dramatic?" She lifted the pen to her notebook, ready for any tidbits I could give her. "This is your chance to share Desi's side of the story. If I can get my piece in today, we'll be able to scoop the *Seattle Times*."

"I think you need to leave now. I need to pick up my son from school." I opened the door but paused on the threshold. "Desi would never hurt anyone."

"Then how do you explain Samuel Westen being poisoned before he fell or was shoved off that cliff by his house? And a box of Desi's signature brownies being found at his house? The police seem to think that makes her a pretty good suspect." Niely flashed me another smile and shoved her business card at me before hobbling down the front steps to an aging Buick.

I shut the door without another word and collapsed into an armchair in our living room. The stiff pillow of the formal brocade-covered chair dug into my back, but I hardly noticed. Mr. Westen had been poisoned. He'd been fine when I'd last seen him, so it must have happened after I brought him the brownies. Crap. I'd brought him the brownies. Did their whole case hinge on a box of baked goods? Now I really regretted being nice to him.

I had to tell Tomàs I'd delivered the brownies to Mr. Westen. If the police knew I'd brought him the brownies, they would have to take Desi off the suspect list. But where did that leave me? It didn't matter—the important thing was they would leave her alone.

14

Guilt over the brownie fiasco rattled around in my head like rocks in a tumbler. Before leaving to pick up the kids at school, I slugged down two Ibuprofen to quell the pain before the boys' antics made it worse.

My plan for preschool pickup was to get in and get out with the least amount of contact possible with Nancy Davenport. Unfortunately, I'd neglected to let the boys in on my plan. I herded Anthony and Mikey to the front door and was almost home free when Mikey remembered something.

"Mom," he said, tugging at my hand.

"What?"

He pulled me toward the back of the school and stopped in front of the classroom gerbils' cage.

"Isn't he cool?" His face beamed. "His name is Spice and the other one is Sugar." It seemed to me a gerbil was just a fancy name for a mouse, but the kids seemed to like them. I liked them just fine when they were stuck behind a layer of terrarium glass.

"Oh, wow. Yep, he's pretty cool." I looked around the

room and didn't see Nancy anywhere. I still had a chance. "Well, let's go."

"No, Mom, you need to talk to Miss Nancy. It's my turn to have Sugar and Spice over the weekend, and she said she has to show you how to take care of them first."

He had to be kidding. I was supposed to purposefully have rodents staying overnight in my house? But if I didn't take them, Mikey would be crushed and the PTA Queen Bees would have more ammunition against me. I looked at the wall calendar. It was only Wednesday, so I had a few days to figure out how to get out of this.

"Uh..." I said. Mike looked up at me expectantly.

"Honey, let's talk about this later."

"No, now!" Mikey shouted. The other children stopped chattering to listen. "I want to take them home. You never let me take them home. Everyone else gets to, and it's my turn now." His face had turned bright red, and his lips were set in a firm line as he stared up at me.

I stared back at him. What had gotten into my sweet little boy? Out of the corner of my eye, I saw Nancy making a beeline for us, her progress slowed by children playing on the floor.

"Mikey, we'll talk about this later."

Anthony tugged at my hand. "Aunt Jill? I have to go potty."

Judging by the wetness that seeped down the front of his pants, it was a little late. I grabbed a pouting Mikey, and together we took Anthony into the bathroom and changed him into his emergency pants.

By the time we were finished, Nancy had her back turned to us, helping a child at the sink. I ushered the kids through the back door before she realized we were done in the bathroom. It wasn't until the glass door thudded behind us that I began to breathe normally. Luckily, in all the commotion, Mikey seemed to have forgotten temporarily about his sharp-toothed would-be houseguests.

I brought the kids to Tomàs and Desi's house, stopping to buy a couple of pizzas on the way. Desi was the primary cook and grocery shopper in the family, and I would be shocked if there was anything besides condiments left in their fridge. I'd called to let Beth know I'd be late to pick up Ella, and she'd assured me she was happy to spend more time with her granddaughter. I waited until the boys were happily watching a Disney movie in the other room before I told Tomàs about Niely's visit and the real origin of the brownies.

"Jill, calm down." Tomàs leaned his arms on the kitchen table and rested his forehead on his hands. He looked up. "Well, this explains a lot. I didn't think Desi would have brought him any brownies after that dust-up at the town council meeting, but with the baby and all, I didn't want to ask."

"So she's clear now?"

"The team that's investigating isn't sharing everything with me, but a buddy of mine said Westen was poisoned by Digal, some sort of heart medicine. They don't know how he was poisoned though. Samples from the house are still in testing." He stood and grabbed a light jacket. "This is such a mess. Even with the brownies coming from you, I don't know if that will get them off Desi as a suspect. I have to admit, she did come at him at the council meeting. But she'd never kill anyone. Can you watch the kids for a bit? I'm going to go down to the station and let them know about the brownies."

I nodded, relieved to know this was out of my hands and

Desi would appear less guilty to the police than she had before.

"And this will clear her?" I twisted a paper napkin between my fingers.

"No." Tomàs frowned. "That's the trouble with poison. It could have been planted in his kitchen weeks ago, and he just now consumed whatever it was. Or someone could have spiked his coffee the morning he died. We won't know anything until the lab reveals how Westen was poisoned. But this will help. At least they won't have a direct link between Desi and the murder."

After he left, I cleared the pizza boxes and the shredded remains of my napkin from the table. I'd hoped Desi wouldn't be a suspect after the truth was known about the box of brownies, but it didn't sound like it would clear her. I prayed she wouldn't find out she was still a suspect. She needed to keep the baby nice and safe for many more weeks. To hedge my bets on prayer, I planned to continue digging into Mr. Westen's affairs on my own. A man as nasty and disliked as he was had to have skeletons in his closet that would lead the police away from Desi.

15

Adam had a client dinner in Chicago on Saturday, and he'd be there for the next week, leaving me to be a single parent for awhile. Beth and Lincoln had volunteered to take our kids and Anthony on Friday night, so when I woke up on Saturday morning, I had the house to myself. After turning on the coffee pot, I plucked the newspaper off the hydrangea bush that still bore a hole from last weekend's newspaper. On the deck, I kicked back in a patio chair and savored the aroma of life-giving coffee from the mug I clutched in my hands. As I pulled the paper out of its rain resistant plastic bag to start the crossword puzzle, my cell phone vibrated on the glass-topped table.

"Hello," I said. I didn't recognize the number.

"Jill?" Gena's voice came over the line. "I had to call you from the phone in my hotel room because my phone is dying, and I think I left the charger in the rental car downstairs. It's always such a pain to get anything out of the car, what with the valet parking and all." She paused, "Are you ok? When we spoke last, you hung up so abruptly and you didn't call back. This is the first chance I've had to check in with you."

"Gena, hi." With everything that had happened in the last few days, I had completely forgotten to call her back after Goldie discovered Mr. Westen's body. "Sorry about that. You'll never believe what happened." I told her about the murder and the police suspecting my sister-in-law.

"Yeah, I heard about it on the news. I never thought I'd see sleepy little Ericksville on CNN, much less find out that it is the scene of two murders. But it never occurred to me that you were involved with any of it."

"Wait, two murders?"

"Your neighbor and the guy in that condo fire."

I opened the newspaper and saw the headline on the bottom half of the front page. "Man killed in arson fire."

"They showed the high-rise condo building on the news. Wait, hold on." Gena muffled the phone, and I could hear her instructing someone to put her tray on the table. "Sorry about that, room service just came with my lunch. Where was I? Oh yes, that condo. It's huge! How the heck did they get approved to build that in Ericksville? It towered over everything else in town. No wonder someone set fire to it. It's a shame they would allow that monstrosity in such a cute little town."

"You know, I thought that at first, but I talked with the owner about it and they have a great vision for it to help revitalize downtown," I said, taking a sip of my coffee. I could hear Gena doing the same on her end. "So what exciting locale are you in now? You know I like to live vicariously through you. I haven't been out of the Northwest in over a year." I purposefully omitted the detail about the marketing job at the condo complex. I wanted to give the job she had referred me to a fair chance, and the condo job wouldn't be a long-term thing anyways—if it even got started.

"In Baltimore. This heat is stifling." She crunched on something away from the phone. "Sorry about eating on the phone, but I've got to get to the airport in an hour, and I wanted to eat something first. Did you give any more thought to the job I mentioned before? You'd be so perfect for it."

"I'm sorry, I haven't had much time to think about it. This week has gone by so fast."

"Tell me about it. I've been to three major cities in the last week. I'd give anything to be home right now."

I looked around me. It was pretty nice sitting on my deck in the early morning, with my garden blooming below and the waters of Puget Sound shimmering in the distance.

"So how much travel does this job you mentioned involve?" I felt both excited and queasy at the thought of business travel.

"Not as much as my job, but I would think at least a week a month." Dishes clanked against plastic in the background. "Would that work with the kids? Can Adam watch them when you're gone?"

"I don't know," I admitted. "Adam's been spending a lot of time at work lately, and it doesn't seem to be letting up."

"Well, there are always nannies. Wait. I know someone who's moving out of the area, and they have a fantastic nanny. My friend is always raving about her. She and her husband both travel frequently for work, and the nanny is sometimes home with their daughter for weeks at a time. Do you want my friend's number?"

I felt even more ill at the prospect of leaving my kids for a week, much less a few weeks. But I also felt sick thinking about giving up a possible job opportunity.

"Sure, give me the number."

Gena read the digits off to me, and I scribbled them down on the newspaper.

"Oh, jeez, I've got to run. Let me know about the job as soon as you decide. I need to let them know something ASAP."

I agreed and hung up the phone.

I pulled my legs up onto the chair and hugged my knees, staring at the scenery without actually seeing it. If I didn't accept this job interview, I wasn't sure Gena would be back with more offers. I decided it wouldn't hurt to interview for the job. But was it really what I wanted?

16

I wasn't due at my in-laws to get the kids until after noon, so I took a luxuriously long, hot shower. When my skin was bright pink and pruny, I hiked down the hill to the bookstore to pick up the new mystery novel I'd pre-ordered. Beach Reads was an indie bookseller located next to Elmer's Sea of Fish and was popular with tourists, commuters, and locals. I stopped to check out the rack of sale books outside the door, ducking to avoid hitting my head on a hanging planter. An elderly man sat on the bench below the window with his English bulldog, reading a book and drinking a cup of coffee.

At this time of day, the bookstore was a silent oasis. Jenny Adler, the proprietor, greeted me when the door chimed. I waved hello, and she sat back down on her stool behind the wooden counter and buried her head in a book. It looked like the latest Stephen King novel that Adam had been eyeing. At the back of the shop, a few people stood in line at the espresso counter, and I joined them to get my second fix of the day.

With a latte in hand, I perused the shelves in search of a

new series I hadn't read. I was reading an excerpt out of the middle of one particularly interesting book involving a circus when someone tapped me on the shoulder. I reluctantly looked up from a riveting description of a monkey's involvement in a murderous deception.

"Brenda, hi," I said, putting the book in my shopping basket, along with a few other cozy mysteries off the shelf and the book I'd pre-ordered. It would probably end up in my to-be-read pile for the next year, but I couldn't pass up circus monkeys.

"Hi, how are you? Where are the kids?" Brenda asked. As usual, she looked fabulously put together. I surreptitiously pulled my Lycra tank top down over the yoga pants I'd worn to the store. I'd rationalized the yoga mom look this morning by telling myself I was getting exercise by walking into town.

"I'm child-free this morning, so I'm trying to get in some 'me' time." I sipped my rapidly chilling drink. "What about you?"

"Brad has the kids, so I have a whole child-free weekend." Brenda smiled. "That's the best thing about joint custody. I get to see the kids all week and by the time they're driving me bonkers, I send them off to their Dad's house. Just kidding... well, partly kidding. I love those little goobers, but the free time is nice. I was just picking up a book for Sara and Dara. They've been begging me for this book Ms. Shana read them and they were out of it at the library." She held up a popular kid's picture book.

"No worries, I totally get what you mean." I took another long sip of my drink.

"Hey, if you aren't doing anything else at the moment, would you be interested in coming with me to see a house? It's an older house out in the boonies and, I have to admit, it kind of gives me the creeps to be there alone. I wouldn't mind having someone join me. I need to take some pictures to put up on the MLS online."

"Sure, sounds good. I love to look at houses." As much as I loved my sister-in-law, I needed a break from worrying about her and thinking about Mr. Westen's murder. Brenda and I paid for our books and walked outside to where she'd parallel parked her sparkling white BMW.

"How do you keep this car so clean?" With all the mud we had in the Pacific Northwest, I couldn't fathom having a white car. The inside had retained its new car smell, and the leather seats were unmarred by sticky, jelly-covered fingers.

"I keep it in the garage and don't let the kids near it." Brenda laughed. "I only use this car for work so that it looks good for clients. Got to keep up the image, even with munchkins. You should see my minivan." She made a face. "That thing has seen better days."

"Any chance you and Adam looking for a new place? A few really nice ones just came on the market this week. Nice views too. Although, you have a pretty nice view yourself," Brenda said. We drove down the highway for about fifteen minutes, and she halted at a stop sign. After craning her head from side to side, she made a sharp left turn onto a gravel road.

"No, we're there to stay. It's our forever home. I just like to look. There's such a variety of houses around here. I'd love to live in one of those vintage Craftsman houses, but I'm happy to not have the maintenance expenses that come along with them," I said. "Where are we? Are we still in Ericksville?"

The distance between houses had increased, and there weren't any houses near where we'd turned off on the gravel lane. One side of the road was heavily forested, while the other side was a weed-choked pasture, bordered by a torn barbed wire fence.

"We're on the outskirts of Ericksville. Or as the listing will say, 'Quaint country setting close to the city'." Brenda grinned at me and expertly piloted the car into a parking spot that had been consumed by weeds. I stepped out of the car and took a long look at the house.

"Yuck. How long has this house been empty?" The farmhouse's yellow paint had peeled off in large chunks, and someone had boarded up the windows bordering the front porch, which drooped in places.

"About five years. The owner is in a nursing home and only recently gave her daughter permission to put the house on the market." Brenda climbed the steps and unlocked the front door with the key from the lockbox attached to the handle.

"It doesn't look like they've performed any maintenance for years before that." I followed her into the unkempt house.

"The owner and her husband lived here for sixty years together, but he passed away and then she went into the nursing home, so you're probably right." Brenda wrinkled her nose. "It doesn't look like I'll be taking pictures anytime soon. We've got to get a cleaning crew in here first." She withdrew a Kleenex from her purse and wiped a clean circle on the kitchen window. "Nice woods view. This house just needs a little touch-up, and someone will snap it right up."

"A little touch-up? What this place needs is a bulldozer." I gingerly made my way across the cracked vinyl floor to where Brenda stood.

"You don't watch many of the home makeover reality shows, do you? People really go for these vintage homes. Look, it's the original farmhouse sink," she said, turning on the faucet. A loud *thunk* reverberated throughout the kitchen, and brown water spurted out of the faucet. Brenda quickly turned it off. "Ok, so maybe it could use more than a touch-up."

"Have you been inside the house before?"

"Just once, about a year ago, but then the owner decided she wasn't ready to sell yet." Brenda took a notebook out of her purse and made notes. Snapping it shut, she said, "Let's take a look upstairs. I'd like to get a repair crew in here to take care of everything all at once so we can get this on the market."

"Is it safe?" I looked dubiously at the orange shag carpeted stairs, which reminded me of the carpet at Mr. Westen's. At least part of the house had been updated in the seventies. The rest appeared to be original issue from the twenties.

"Of course. These houses were built to last. Not like the cheap junk they build nowadays." Brenda led the way up the pumpkin-colored staircase and paused at the top of the stairs. "Look at this hand-carved banister. These are the kinds of details that will sell the house." She rubbed her fingers lightly over the woodwork and then brushed her hands together to get rid of the dust coating them.

We entered a sparsely furnished bedroom with hardwood floors. Cobwebs hung like cloaks from the corners, and I spotted mouse poop scattered over the top of a bookshelf. I regretted following Brenda up the stairs.

"I think I'll head back down," I said, backing out of the room.

"No wait, I want to show you one of the other bedrooms." She brushed past me and pushed open another door at the top of the landing. "I thought it was in here."

Brenda strode over to a dresser that was built into an alcove under the eaves.

"How cool is this? A lot of these old houses have built-ins like this. Houses used to be built smaller, and they really knew how to maximize space." She knelt down on the dusty hardwood floor and tugged on the bottom drawer. Reaching under the drawer, she pulled down what had appeared to be a fixed base of the dresser, but was actually a board on hinges.

"See?" Her words bubbled out as she turned to me. "They built a secret compartment in here. People used to hide their jewelry and other valuables in some of the built-ins because you can't see the hidden section just by looking at it."

I had to admit it was pretty cool. "Do they have built-ins in all the rooms?"

"No, I think I saw one in the dining room, but this is the only one I remember upstairs." Brenda's brow furrowed over immaculately tweezed eyebrows. "Wait. I think there is one in the bathroom."

We both crowded into the small upstairs bathroom. A tall person wouldn't be able to use the shower crammed under the eaves. It would probably be labeled as 'cozy' when Brenda listed the house. The bathroom smelled faintly of mildew but appeared to be in good condition.

"I feel like I'm in a Hostess Sno Ball," I said, looking around the bathroom. Roses adorned the wallpaper, and the Formica countertop was speckled with gold and pink. Even the toilet was made of a matching pink porcelain.

"Go stand by the window," said Brenda. I did as directed.

Brenda shut the white wooden door, revealing a built-in linen closet behind it with three drawers underneath. She tugged on the handle of one of the drawers, and the aroma of cedar wafted out. I breathed in deeply.

"I need one of those. I love the smell of cedar," I said.

"Me too. It always reminds me of walking in the woods with my grandfather when I was a kid. I make do with cedar blocks in my drawers at home, but it's not quite the same as a cedar-lined drawer." She reached for the larger, closet portion of the built-in, but it didn't open. Brenda lightly thumped on the wood to loosen it.

A streak of gray darted out from a hole between the bathtub and the closet.

"Aaaaaahhhhhh!" It took me awhile to realize that the scream was coming from me.

Mickey Mouse's cousin ran directly toward me, its beady little eyes intent on crawling up my pant legs. I panicked and did the first thing that came to mind.

When I opened my eyes, Brenda looked up at me, amused. "You can come down from there. I must have scared it with all the noise, but it's gone now."

I looked down from where I stood on the very pink toilet and sheepishly dismounted. "Uh, I have this thing about mice. They're so creepy with their little tails and ability to get into tiny spaces."

"You wouldn't last long in my business. When houses stand empty, rodents tend to move in. I have an exterminator on speed dial." She grinned at my discomfort, and we walked toward the front door. "So this house hasn't exactly convinced you to move, huh?" She locked the front door, and we started down the steps. I couldn't get away from the Mouse House fast enough.

"Haha." I laughed good-naturedly. "No, I'm staying put. Adam and I searched for years for the perfect house for us, and we found it."

Brenda grew more serious. "With all those houses going in below you, you might change your mind. Living with construction noise for a few years would make me want to move."

"What houses? What construction?" I asked, stopping abruptly on the final step.

"You didn't know? I figured there was some sort of notification process before a lot could be subdivided to that extent."

"Brenda, what are you talking about?" Blood pounded in my ears. I was afraid I already knew the answer.

"Samuel Westen was selling his house and land. I spoke with the developer, Elliott Elkins, about it last week. We both attended the same continuing education class. Ericksville has a pretty small real estate community, so we all know each other. He asked me to be the sales agent for the development." Brenda fiddled with her car keys. "I'm sorry, I really thought you knew."

"No, I didn't," I said through clenched teeth. Even in death, Samuel Westen was reaching from behind the grave to mess with my family. "How many houses are we talking about?"

"Twenty-four houses, I believe."

"Twenty-four? Holy cow. How are they going to get that many houses on his few acres?" It was unfathomable to think of the woods below our house being mowed down for an entire subdivision.

"It's going to be one of those developments where the houses are really close together and have a common area between them. They euphemistically call them 'cottage homes,' but it's really an excuse to cram as many houses as possible into a plot of land. It will be a fantastic opportunity for me though. How many major developments do we get in

Ericksville? I can almost taste the twins' college fund." Brenda didn't seem to notice how upset I felt.

"How the heck did they get that past the zoning board?" We didn't have an HOA, but the city of Ericksville tended to be conservative when it came to lot sizes.

"Do you really have to ask? Your neighbor had some powerful connections."

"You're right. That's going to be miserable. Any chance it didn't go through before his death?"

"I don't know." Brenda shook her head and slid into the driver's seat. I collapsed into the passenger seat.

"I suppose there's a chance, but Elliott seemed pretty sure the deal would go through," she said.

"I spoke with Samuel Westen's daughter yesterday, and she didn't say anything about him selling the property." I remembered Anna's vehement opposition to the idea of her father selling the BeansTalk Café property. I couldn't imagine how mad she would be if she knew about his intentions to sell her mother's home.

"Maybe she didn't know about it?"

"I guess. I still can't believe it." I felt like the seatbelt restraint was going to crush my chest. I opened my window to let in some fresh air. "I know this deal is important to you, but if there's a chance it didn't go through, I'm going to fight it. Maybe there is some legal loophole with his death."

"I don't blame you one bit. I wouldn't want it in my neighborhood either, but if they are going to be built anyway, I might as well be the one selling them," Brenda said. She executed a three-point turn in the driveway and drove away from the house, her wheels churning up the gravel as we sped back to the main road.

Brenda dropped me off at my house a half hour before I needed to leave to meet my mother-in-law at the Boathouse.

Before I left home, I looked out the window at the Westen place. How was it possible for one man to cause so much pain to others? I'd put so much time and effort into finding this house and had dreamed of raising my family here on this quiet street. Now there could be twenty-four more families living below us, creating noise and additional traffic, and ruining our view. Development of the Westen property would decrease the property value of our home, as well as our joy in living there.

17

I found Beth in her office at the Boathouse, making decorations. She waved at me from behind a mound of pink- and lime-green bows. Ella smiled at me from her Exersaucer next to her grandmother.

"What are these for?" I asked.

"They're for an upcoming wedding in the main hall."

"So was the bride on some sort of drugs when she chose these colors?" The neon shades hurt my eyes. "They look like some sort of flashback to the 1980s."

"You should see the bride." Beth waggled her eyebrows and grinned at me. "I'm curious to see what her wedding dress looks like. When we last spoke, there was talk of a pink and green veil and matching train. She's an artist, very eclectic."

"Do you need help?" I eyed the pile of silky wide ribbon Beth was fashioning into bows.

"I have two hundred and fifty of these to make. I will babysit for a week if you help me get these done before my eyes are burned from the neon glow they emit," Beth said.

I took a seat at the round table in her office. "Actually,

about the babysitting. Remember the client event intake meeting for the Boathouse I had on Saturday?"

"Yes, something about a class reunion?" Beth's fingers stopped in mid-bow, and she furrowed her brow. "Was that for late summer?"

"Yep, that's the one." I tossed a finished bow on the pile and grabbed more ribbons to twist. "The client kind of offered me a job."

"Jill, that's wonderful. Did you take it? What will you be doing?"

"I said I'd do it. It's not a big deal, only a few hours a week, but it would get me back into the business. I'd be creating and implementing a marketing plan for the condos down by the water. I was hoping you'd watch Ella for a couple of hours on Monday when I start the job."

"Of course I will." Beth frowned. "But the condos that caught on fire? You aren't going to be the most popular person around town."

"I know, but they're going to be built anyways. This could be really good for me. A friend of mine referred me for a full-time marketing position, but I don't think this is the right time for that with Adam being gone so much and all."

Beth was quiet for a moment. "Jill, I know I shouldn't say this with Adam being my son, but if this is something you're interested in pursuing, he's going to have to figure out a way for both of you to get the careers you want. But only if it's what you really want. And there's always an opening for you at the Boathouse. Just think about it and let us know. Lincoln and I will be here to support you and Adam with whatever you decide."

"I will. But for right now, I've got bigger fish to fry. Has

Desi said anything to you lately about the BeansTalk building being sold?"

"She hasn't talked about it much with everything going on. The last time she mentioned it was when we attended the town council meeting." She turned serious. "I hope with his passing that it's no longer an issue?"

"I don't know. I spoke with Samuel Westen's daughter, Anna, about it. I think you know her? She used to work at the Boathouse. Anyways, she is against selling the Beans-Talk building, but we found some paperwork indicating it may be too late. She's checking with her attorney."

"Yes, I know Anna. We volunteer together at the Ericksville Historical Society." Beth leaned back in her office chair and looked up at me. "Please don't tell Desi. I don't think she can handle that right now. I may have led her to believe that everything was going to be ok with the lease."

"Sure. I won't mention it to her. But it gets worse. My friend, who's a real estate agent in town, just told me Samuel Westen planned to sell the land his own house sits on for one of those mega developments. I had no idea he'd even planned it."

Beth shook her head. "That's old Samuel. Rotten to the core and not caring about anyone else."

"No kidding. The more I learn about the man, the more I realize people must have been lining up at his doorstep to kill him. Heck, at this point, even I have motive to kill him."

"Jill, don't say that. The police already suspect Desi—this family can't take much more. What did Adam say about Westen's land being developed?"

"I haven't had a chance to tell him yet. I just found out today, and he's out of town for work."

"He's been traveling a lot lately," Beth observed, her eyes focused sharply on me. "How are you doing alone with the kids? Do you want to come stay with Lincoln and I? I worry about you alone in that house, especially with Samuel Westen's murder happening right nearby."

"I'm fine, don't worry about us. Remember, I've got Goldie to protect me."

"Hah! Goldie is more likely to lick an intruder to death than anything else."

"True, but really, don't worry. Like I said, practically everyone in town hated Samuel Westen. I don't think there is quite that level of detestation for me," I said wryly. "But in all seriousness, I think I'm more in danger of Mikey driving me crazy. He won't listen to anything I say, and I feel like I've tried everything with him. Amazon is making a mint off of my parenting book orders."

Beth nodded sympathetically. "It will get better. If I learned anything raising four kids, it's that none of the stages last forever. Soon Mikey will be back to being your sweet little boy again. It may not be tomorrow or next week, but it will be here sooner than you think."

Anthony and Mikey shrieked loudly from the other room, cutting off our conversation.

"Boys!" Beth called. "The crew needs to get in there to set up tables for the event tonight. Please come in here." Turning to me, she said, "They play together so nicely. I can't tell you how glad I am that you and Adam decided to settle down in Ericksville."

Mikey and Anthony came running up to us, their faces flushed. "Can we have a drink, Grandma?" Mikey asked.

Beth answered, "Sure honey, there's chocolate milk in the fridge."

"Are you ok with having Anthony here? Aren't you getting ready for an event?" I asked.

Beth looked down at her wristwatch. "Tomàs should be

here soon to get Anthony."

As if on cue, Tomàs poked his head into the office. "Did I hear my name?" He smiled, but beneath his smile, he looked as though he'd aged ten years in the last few days. "Hey, Jill—does Mikey want to spend the night at our house? It's Saturday, so I thought I'd take the boys to see Desi and then bring them back to our house for some Chinese food and a movie. Would that be ok with you? I know having Mikey around would help take Anthony's mind off his mom being in the hospital."

"That's fine with me, but are you sure? I don't want to add to your stress. Mikey can be quite a handful," I said.

"If I can handle breaking up a fight today between two men who were drunker than skunks before noon, I think I can handle two three-year-olds."

"Ok, do you need anything for him? He'll probably fit in a pair of Anthony's pajamas. Don't forget to put a Pull-Up on him at night. And he likes to have the light on for a few minutes before he falls asleep."

"Jill, don't worry, he'll be fine."

"Tomàs," I whispered urgently, not wanting the boys to hear, "what did they say down at the station about Desi and the brownies?"

"I told the guys in charge of the investigation. They don't have the results back from the lab yet, so they're still not sure how Westen was poisoned. I don't know much more. But, Jill? Don't say anything to Desi about any of it."

I nodded.

"Mikey, Anthony, let's go," Tomàs hollered down the hallway. The boys peeked around the corner.

"What, Dad?" Anthony asked.

"It's time to go home," Tomàs said. He turned to Mikey. "Mikey, your mom said you could spend the night with us.

What movie do you want to see?" The boys cheered and ran to Tomàs, shouting movie suggestions in their little high-pitched voices as the three of them went out the door together.

Without the boys, the office was so silent I could hear the refrigerator running in the kitchen on the other side of the wall. Even Ella remained quiet. I picked her up from her Exersaucer and held her on my hip.

"Beth, I have a favor to ask."

"Sure, what's up?" Beth said.

"Samuel Westen's funeral is tomorrow at ten o'clock. Do you think you could watch the kids for an extra two hours so I can go? I feel as though I should attend. After all, he was my neighbor."

"Of course, Jill. No problem. Although he wasn't a very nice man, it's still nice to pay your respects to a neighbor."

"Thanks, Beth. I appreciate it."

I'd only been home long enough to feed Ella a bottle and a jar of pureed carrots when I received a phone call from Anna Westen.

"Anna, it's nice to hear from you. How are you doing?" I asked while wiping orange gunk out of Ella's hair. It amazed me how much area one small container of baby food could cover. She was going to need a bath.

"Hi, Jill. Sorry to bother you, but I was hoping you could do me a favor. When I was over at the house the last time, I noticed the kitchen sink was leaking and the plumber finally has time to come out and fix it."

"Ok, do you need me to let the plumber in?"

"Would you? My son has a baseball game tonight, and

this was the only opening all week the plumber had available."

"When will they be here?"

"In half an hour. Is that ok?"

"Sure, no problem."

"Thanks, I'll call the company and let them know you'll meet them there." Anna gave me the information about the plumbing company and the location of the spare key to her father's house."Thanks, Jill, you're a lifesaver."

"Glad to be able to help. Let me know if there's anything else you need."

I looked down at Ella. She was pretending her hands were windshield wipers, moving food from side to side and swiping it off of the highchair tray. I mopped her up as well as I could and put her in the stroller. Bath time was going to have to wait.

I found the key to the Westen house under the third flowerpot from the door, right where Anna had said it would be. I felt like an intruder, even though I had a key and had been given permission to enter. The house was oddly cold for being shut up in the warm weather. Mr. Westen's ghost was probably haunting his house.

Ella had already fallen asleep in the stroller, so I reclined her seat, put her favorite stuffed bunny on a nearby chair, and turned off the living-room light. From upstairs, a banging noise startled me. Feeling paranoid, I grabbed a knife from the kitchen and tiptoed up the stairs. When I neared the top of the stairs, the cause of the noise became apparent. The window in Mr. Westen's study had been left open and the flimsy vinyl blinds hit the wall with every breeze from outside. I closed the window and rubbed my arms.

Manila file folders on the desk caught my attention. A

bank statement from First Bank of Ericksville poked out of the top folder. Anna must have left everything behind that she didn't need immediately. Curiosity got the best of me. If I wanted to find out who else had a motive to kill Samuel Westen, where better to start than with his biggest love—money. I sat down behind the desk and opened the first file.

A quick survey of his bank statements revealed no surprises. Mr. Westen had been loaded. He didn't need the money from selling his house or Desi's building. Pure greed had been his motivation for those sales. Cancelled checks were rubber-banded and stuck in with the bank statements. I grabbed one set of checks and flipped through them. A series of transactions caught my eye. Donations of fifteen thousand dollars a year to Willowby College, for four years in a row. I looked closer. The last check had been written fifteen years ago. There were also smaller, more recent, charitable donations to the Ericksville Garden Society and various other local charities.

So Mr. Westen wasn't all bad. I had to admit, I'd never thought of him as a particularly generous man. It made me feel better to have some positive impressions of him before I attended his funeral the next day.

His bank statements reflected numerous monthly deposits of around a thousand dollars each, including copies of checks from Desi, which I assumed were lease payments from the buildings in his rental portfolio. A series of deposits had been made for $9,999 a month. What building could that be for? Ericksville wasn't exactly known for its high-rent district. Whatever building it was, he'd received payments for it for the last two years.

I pulled out the wide middle desk drawer. Instead of being filled with pens and papers like I'd expected, it contained candy bars and Jelly Bellys. Ha! Mr. Westen had been a closet candy addict. Tucked in the back of the drawer was a framed photo of Anna and a small boy who I assumed to be her son. My neighbor must have had some sentimentality if he had kept a photo of them in his desk.

I looked around his desk and the file cabinet for the file Anna had pulled out with the real estate documents. I wanted to know if the deal for Westen's house and land had gone through prior to his death. Unfortunately, Anna had removed that particular file. I'd have to ask her what she'd discovered next time I spoke with her.

I brightened. Better yet, I could casually ask Elliott Elkins himself when I saw him after the funeral. I could go right to the source without worrying myself sick about a future development being built below my house.

I looked at the ship's clock on the wall. The plumbers should be at the house in about ten minutes, and I needed to check on Ella. I put the bank statements and checks back in their folders and straightened the files. With luck, Anna wouldn't notice my snooping.

I was about to go down the stairs to Ella when the closed bedroom door at the top of the stairs seemed to call out my name. I opened the door and the smell of must assailed my senses. Mr. Westen hadn't used this room much. Looking around, I could see why.

The room had belonged to Anna's brother. Benton's bedroom didn't look like it had been touched since he died as a teenager. Trophies lined the back of an oak dresser, and posters of rock stars were peeling off the walls. I flipped on the light. A quilted bedspread covered the scarred wooden twin bed. A baseball bat leaned against the wall in the corner of the room. Like other surfaces in the house, dust didn't dare sully the furnishings.

Either someone had cleaned Benton's room after he

died, or he had been the neatest teenager I'd ever seen. I peeked into the closet. It was fully of neatly hung, evenly spaced jeans and T-shirts. The top of the desk held only a pencil cup.

In the corner of the room, under the eaves, was a built-in dresser Brenda would die for. I crossed the room and ran my fingers over the intricate woodwork. She was right. The old houses in this area did have some wonderful original details. I wondered if I could replicate it in my house. In Ella's room, there was an alcove that would be perfect for a built-in dresser.

On impulse, I tapped the bottom of the dresser. It sprang open, revealing a hidden space. It was the ideal place for a teenager to conceal things.

I lay down on the cold wood floor and reached into the hole. At first I didn't feel anything, but then my fingers closed around a thin glass object. I pulled the object out, taking with it a family of dust bunnies. I brushed the picture frame off, revealing a Polaroid photo of a teenage boy with his arm around a pretty girl of about the same age. Had Benton had a girlfriend? Why had he hidden the picture?

Ding-dong! Ding-dong!

The doorbell's chime woke Ella, and she started screaming. I shoved the picture back into the crevice and closed the compartment.

"Coming!" I shouted, getting to my knees and standing creakily. At thirty-four, I was getting too old to be lying down on hard surfaces.

I played with Ella and her stuffed bunny on the living room floor until the plumbers left. It wasn't until I put her to bed at night that I realized I'd left the toy at Mr. Westen's house. I'd have to remember to pick it up after the funeral tomorrow.

18

The sky above the funeral tent was as gray and stormy as the man being buried. There was a surprisingly large turnout for a widely despised man. Anna and her son stood in the front row, garbed in black, directly in front of the closed casket. I held my hand up to wave and smiled at her. She nodded back at me before returning to her discussion with a suited, official-looking man. I squished my way across the damp grass and joined the rest of the mourners gathered at the grave site.

At the back, two men stood ramrod straight, their suit jackets left loose to conceal what I assumed to be holsters. They scanned the crowd discreetly and, every so often, murmured something to one another. I wasn't surprised to see the cops here. I hoped their job would be as simple as the movie scenes where the police catch the murderer hiding behind a tree at their victim's funeral. Somehow I didn't think things happened quite like in the movies.

I craned my neck around to look at a grove of tall alders nearby, but I didn't catch a glimpse of a killer. However, I did see quite a few of Mr. Westen's fellow town council members and the mayor. They posed in front of a tree while a man I presumed to be a photographer from the newspaper snapped their picture.

The sound of a microphone crackled across the grassy knoll.

"Good morning. Thank you all for coming out to celebrate the life of one of our city's most treasured citizens," said the man in clerical robes.

Many people spoke kind words about Samuel Westen, but their words were hollow. I wondered if they even knew him. When it was Anna's turn at the podium, she dabbed at her eyes a few times and gave a poignant speech about her father. His death must have affected her more than she had initially realized.

"Hrmph," someone said under their breath.

I swiveled around. The face of the woman next to me was stony, and she glared at the coffin as though Samuel Westen could see her hatred. The man next to her laid his hand on her arm.

"Gwen," he said quietly. She pushed his hand away.

Shocking. Someone else disliked the dead man. I turned back to the service and shifted my weight from side to side. Standing on the uneven ground in heels was a recipe for sore feet.

After the casket was lowered into the ground, I paid my respects to Anna and her son, whom she introduced as Dylan. He politely shook my hand and thanked me for coming. He had a great deal of poise for his age, especially for someone who had, by Anna's account, been largely ignored by his grandfather.

I walked away from the mourners and was halfway down the hill when my left heel sunk into the ground. I crashed to the ground like a tree being felled.

"Are you ok?" A woman's voice drifted down to me. I wiggled my extremities and determined the only thing wounded was my pride. That and the last pair of run-free pantyhose I owned.

"Yes, thank you." I grabbed her outstretched hand and rose shakily on my miraculously still intact heels.

"Not a great day for heels," the woman observed. I looked at my rescuer. It was the woman who had glared at the casket during the funeral service.

"It's never a great day for heels." I laughed and held out my hand. "Jill Andrews. Thanks for helping me up."

"Gwen Hanson," she said, with a firm handshake.

"I saw you at the service. Was that your husband with you?"

"Yes, that was Harold. He's gone to get the car." She rubbed her knees. "I've developed rheumatoid arthritis and, when I have a flare-up, it's hard for me to get around. But I wasn't going to miss seeing Samuel Westen being buried six feet under."

I must have looked shocked because she said, "Oh, I'm sorry, were you close?"

"No, actually, he was my neighbor and he wasn't very neighborly, if you catch my drift." I'd tried very hard during the funeral service to think positive things about Mr. Westen, but now that he was in the ground, all bets were off. "How did you know him?"

"I've known him for a very long time." Tears pooled in her eyes. Shoot. Maybe I'd misinterpreted her feelings for Mr. Westen.

"Mrs. Hanson—are you ok?" I handed her a tissue from the emergency pack I always kept in my purse.

"Oh, yes. I'm ok now. In fact, the funeral provided the closure I desperately needed." She took a deep breath and smiled through her tears. “Samuel Westen was my high-school boyfriend’s father. One day, Benton, my boyfriend, and his father got into a huge argument. Benton went out with friends to drink it off. The car he was riding in crashed on the way home and he was killed instantly.” She looked at me, as though seeing me for the first time, and gave a little laugh. “I don’t know why I’m telling you this. I’ve never told anyone, other than my husband.”

I smiled at her sympathetically.

“I’m so sorry for your loss. I just met Anna Westen a few days ago, and she told me about losing her brother at such a young age. I can’t imagine how difficult that must have been for you.”

“Yes, well, Samuel Westen made the situation even worse. You see, they were arguing over me. Benton wanted to enlist in the army as soon as he graduated from high school so we could get married, but his father told him he would disinherit him if he did so.”

“From what I heard, Samuel Westen liked to get his way. I doubt Benton even had a chance.”

“Samuel Westen took away the future Benton and I had planned together, as well as our chance to raise our son as a family.”

“Benton had a son? You were pregnant?” I paused. This was starting to sound like an episode out of a soap opera. “Excuse me, I don’t mean to pry.”

“I was two months pregnant when Benton died. He’d just told his father before the accident. But his father didn’t care about the baby. He wanted Benton to go to school and become a lawyer. He saw me and the baby as hindrances to his son’s bright future.”

“So what happened with the baby?”

“Benton’s father gave me fifteen thousand dollars to

leave Ericksville. He threatened to make life miserable for me and my parents if I didn't take it. My dad was just eking out a living as a fisherman, and Samuel Westen had the power to make things difficult for him. I went to live with my older sister in Portland, where I had the baby."

"Why did you never say anything later? From all accounts, your son would have been an heir to a fortune."

"I never wanted to see or speak to Samuel Westen again. And I never did." Gwen laughed hollowly. "I used to dream about killing him for the way he treated Benton."

"Does your son know Samuel Westen was his grandfather?" I couldn't help but pry.

"No, and he never will. I rarely speak of his father, and he's never asked about his father's family," Gwen said. "I didn't come back to Ericksville until I was married and had changed my last name, so Samuel Westen probably never knew I was even here."

She looked at her husband in the distance. He walked toward us and waved. "Harold and I've been married for thirty years now, and I couldn't ask for a better man. We've been through a lot with his heart attack scares and truckloads of daily medications and treatments, but I wouldn't trade our life together for anything. I've tried to forgive Samuel Westen for what he did, but I can't seem to find it in me. Does that make me a bad person?"

I shrugged.

"He's dead now though, and maybe I can finally close that part of my life." She looked at me defiantly. "Benton gave me a wonderful child, and the past can now stay in the past."

~

After my chat with Gwen Hanson, I went back to the car for the flowers I'd bought on the way to the cemetery. I reparked my car in the children's section. I walked directly to a still-new headstone with a small angel perched on top. I lay a small bouquet of daisies in front of the headstone and ran my fingers over the marker. It said simply, "Ariana Torres, beloved daughter and sister."

Memories flooded over me. The call from Tomàs notifying us that Desi was in the hospital. The prayers that their little girl could survive when she was born just shy of twenty-three weeks, and the devastation when she passed away soon after birth.

Tears rolled down my face before I could get to my emergency Kleenex pack. I would never forgive myself for not helping Desi out more. We knew she was having a difficult pregnancy and, if only she had taken it easier, maybe she could have kept Ariana inside longer. I was newly pregnant with Ella and suffering from morning sickness, along with taking care of Mikey, but I should have helped more. I wasn't going to let anything happen this time.

A woman a few gravesites over smiled at me through tears of her own. "You never forget the loss of a child. It hurts less over time, but it never completely goes away."

I nodded and swiped at my eyes with a Kleenex. Walking past the woman, I read the gravestone above where she was planting a flower and noticed the child had been only two years old. When I got home, I was going to hug my babies tight. Although Mikey and Ella could be a handful, I was grateful for them every day.

19

In all the chaos surrounding Samuel Westen's death and funeral, I'd almost forgotten I'd promised to start my new job the next day. Would there even be any marketing to do for the condo project? With the extent of the fire damage, I wasn't sure the condo building project could be salvaged. Elliott must be devastated by the arson. I decided to call him to check if he still wanted me to come in.

"Hi Elliott, it's Jill Andrews."

"Oh, hello Jill, it's good to hear from you. Are you planning on coming in tomorrow at ten?" He sounded as though nothing had happened.

"I wasn't sure if you still needed me. With the fire and... um, everything."

"Yes, well, it's been difficult." Elliott cleared his throat. "I'm sorry, Jill. I need to take a call on the other line. I'll see you tomorrow? We've temporarily moved into a construction trailer next to the building."

"Definitely. I'll be there with bells on. See you tomorrow." I hung up the phone and hit myself over the head with it. With bells on? I spent way too much time with the under-five crowd.

The next day, I woke up early to get ready before I woke up the kids. For the second time in two days, I put on foundation, lipstick, and mascara. I wound my hair into a neat bun and added jewelry I normally wouldn't dare to wear around grabby baby hands. I put on the gray slacks that had been a favorite in my past life as a marketing manager. I had to lay flat on the bed to fasten the button, and I prayed it wouldn't pop off. It was time to cut back on chocolate.

Mikey wandered into our bedroom with pajamas still on and his face flushed from sleep. "Mommy, you look different." He wrinkled up his face and stared at me. "Did someone else die?"

"No, sweetie, no one died. I'm just wearing nice clothes for work." I did a pirouette in front of the mirror and was satisfied with my reflection.

I threw my bathrobe on over my dress clothes to keep them clean until we left and got both kids dressed and fed. I'd almost made it to the car without incident when Ella spit up all over her onesie. I got her changed into a clean outfit and put her in her car carrier. After getting both kids into their car seats and sliding into my own seat, I noticed I hadn't escaped Ella's mess. I used a baby wipe to clean off the trace of spit-up and told myself it was unnoticeable on the black fabric of my blouse.

The morning drop-off routine went by in a blur, and soon I stood in front of the Sunset Avenue condo project. The acrid scent of smoke still hung in the air. The fire had only affected the west end of the building. Seagulls sat on scaffolding, surveying the charred remains. It seemed like considerably more than a week ago that I'd seen Perry Winston stride confidently through the construction site.

A trailer labeled "Office" had been set up in the parking lot.

It had been a long time since I'd worked in a professional setting. Before I reached the door, I gave myself a pep talk. It was going to be ok, and I was going to rock this job, out of practice or not. I wiped sweaty palms on my pants and gazed at the ocean for a minute before I knocked on the door of Elkins Development Group.

"Come in." Elliott's deep voice came through the door. I pushed it open. It smelled like air freshener in the trailer. I wrinkled my nose.

"I know. Awful, isn't it? But it's better than smelling smoke all day," Elliott said.

He looked a decade older than when I'd seen him a week before. His tan had faded, and his skin looked sallow underneath. Even his clothes seemed to hang on his limbs. He strode over to me and shook my hand with limp fingers.

"Good to see you again," Elliott said graciously.

"It's good to be here." I scanned the room. "This is actually pretty nice for a trailer. Did everything in the old office burn in the fire?"

"No, but the office reeked of smoke, so I had the construction crew move everything salvageable out here."

"How's Perry doing? He seemed rather upset last time I was here. This must be so difficult for both of you."

"He hasn't seen the fire damage." A sad expression crossed Elliott's face before he regained composure. I couldn't imagine how painful it must be to have your life's work go up in smoke.

"Perry flew to Baltimore the night before the fire to meet with his ex-wife. He was so invested in the project, it will just kill him to see it." He sat down behind his desk.

"I'm sure," I murmured sympathetically

"Nothing to do now but move on. The insurance money should cover everything, and we can rebuild." He shuffled papers around on his desk.

"Would you like something to drink before we get started?"

"That would be great," I said.

He stood and I waved at him to sit back down.

"I can get it myself. Remember, I work for you now."

Looking around the room, I found the beverage station. Whereas in Elliott's office in the condo building, the drinks had been in their own little alcove, here they were crammed into a corner. Six water glasses were stacked in front of a crystal pitcher and the beveled crystal Scotch decanter with matching glasses.

I poured myself a glass of water from the crystal pitcher and turned to him. "Would you like anything?" He shook his head. I motioned to the Scotch. "This set is beautiful. Where did you get it from? My husband would love it."

He held his fingers to his lips. "Shh. Don't tell anyone, but I got it from Bed Bath & Beyond for half off. I wanted a little something new to make the place cheerier. What do you think of the painting over there?" He pointed at a landscape of the Ericksville Lighthouse at sunset. The pink and orange sky was set off nicely by the freshly painted peach-colored walls of the trailer.

"It's beautiful. Was that from the same store?" I asked. A satisfied smile replaced Elliott's sad expression.

"It's from the Ericksville Art Gallery. Also on sale. I learned the art of savvy shopping from my mother."

Who would have thought Elliott Elkins was a closet bargain shopper? Had he been the decorator for the original office space? I asked him and he replied in the affirmative. Elliott was full of surprises.

"Does your mother live in this area?" I gestured to the picture of his parents he'd shown me on my first visit. I moved closer to the picture to get a better look at it and did a double take. I sucked in my breath. It was the same picture I'd found in the hidden compartment in Benton Westen's room. Either it was a very popular stock photo for frames, or Elliott Elkins was Benton's son. But Elliott had said his father was killed in an accident in the army—which sounded as if he didn't have a clue about who his father really was. I glanced at the other photo, a recent shot of Gwen and Harold, which confirmed my suspicion about his parentage.

"Yes, she and my stepdad live in Ericksville. We moved back here when I was fairly young to be close to her family. My father's family had all moved away by the time we returned to Ericksville. My mother met Harold when she was his waitress at a Denny's." He gestured to the picture of them. "They've been married over thirty years now. In fact, they just returned from an anniversary trip to Hawaii." He reached into his desk drawer and pulled out a tray of chocolate-covered macadamia nuts. "Would you like one? Mom brought me some back to thank me for housesitting while they were gone."

"Thanks, I love these things." I took one and hoped he'd offer another, but he closed the box and returned it to the drawer. Too late, I remembered my vow to eat less candy. The desk drawer full of candy reminded me of his grandfather's candy drawer. Anna had a nephew and her son had a cousin. I had a feeling they would be overjoyed to know they had more family. It was too bad Elliott didn't know the truth about his father, and if his mother hadn't ever told him, it certainly wasn't going to be me who spilled the beans.

I pointed to the photo of Gwen and Harold. "Sometimes

I can't believe what a small town this is. I think I may have met your mother. I was at the cemetery yesterday for a funeral and there was woman named Gwen there who looks exactly like her."

Elliott looked up sharply. "Yes, my mother's name is Gwen. What a coincidence. I didn't realize she'd experienced a loss. I'll have to call her later." He then looked at me, as though realizing that I too had been in attendance at the funeral.

"Would it be better to reschedule our meeting for another day? Was the funeral for someone you were close to?"

"No, just a neighbor. In fact, I believe you knew him—Samuel Westen."

"I can't say I knew him well. We'd spoken a few times over the years, but not recently," Elliott said. I looked at him oddly.

"I thought you were working with him on a new multi-home development? Mr. Westen was selling his house and a few acres. Up on Cedar Street?"

"No," Elliott shrugged. "Must have been someone else. I know the property you're talking about, but no, I haven't been up that way in years. It would be a great property though." He looked deep in thought and dollar signs formed in his eyes. "It could be developed with several houses on the parcel while still keeping the manor feel for the main house. If I put in some tall hedges surrounding the English gardens, it wouldn't even feel like it had been subdivided into smaller lots. The manicured gardens and stone benches are a great selling feature for the house. Do you know if his heirs plan on selling?"

"No, sorry, I don't know. I thought Brenda Watkins said you'd spoken with her about being the listing agent for the houses once they were developed, but I must have been mistaken." I knew I hadn't misunderstood Brenda, so why was Elliott lying?

"Must be. I've got my hands full with this project right now. But I'd love to develop that property after this one is complete. Have a seat here." He rotated one of his two computer monitors toward me and pointed to the screen. "I want a website like this one. And," he pushed a brochure toward me, "something like this to send to prospective clients and have on hand for walk-ins."

I nodded, picking up the brochure and opening it. "I think this will work really well for you. I can put together some copy and have a photographer take some pictures of the view. I don't think now is a good time to take pictures of the building." I shuddered a little thinking about the fire-ravaged structure. Not something you wanted prospective owners to see. "Do you have an artist's rendering of what the completed condo building will look like? Maybe something with landscaping too?"

Elliott nodded. "We have this." He pulled a file folder out of a cabinet and spread the contents on the table.

"It's beautiful," I said truthfully. The drawing reflected decidedly Northwest-style architecture with exposed wooden beams, mature landscaping, and pathways. The first floor offered small shops and restaurants, with parking underground. Families with small children sat around wrought-iron tables at an outdoor patio café, licking ice cream cones. A golden retriever that could have been Goldie's brother waited patiently for his owners to finish their treats. Everyone was smiling and happy. Behind the condo, the Willowby Island ferry chugged in to the dock.

"I want to live here," I said, admiring the drawing.

Elliott smiled. "I know. I do as well. This is why we have

to move forward with construction, even with everything that's happened. I realize this building isn't popular, but it could be the future of the downtown area. We're not trying to push out the small businesses. In fact, we're providing affordable spaces for people to lease."

"Well, we'll definitely have to focus on that, but it's going to take more than ice cream to convince people that it's worth blocked views and the additional traffic the condo complex will bring to downtown Ericksville."

"That's what you're here for. To make people realize this is a step in the right direction for the revitalization of downtown."

"Do you mind if I stay here for awhile to look over these images?"

"You can have a seat right over there." He pointed to a small table against the far wall.

I scooped everything we'd been reviewing off the desk, brought the materials over to the side table, and pulled up a chair.

"Just let me know if you have any questions," Elliott said.

"Thanks." I took a notebook out of my bag and jotted down a few notes. A little thrill shot through me. I wasn't completely convinced that this condo complex was the right step for Ericksville as I was rather fond of the current cozy feel of downtown. But progress would happen whether I approved or not, and it was exciting to be a part of it. And, this was one hundred percent better than creating marketing materials extolling the virtues of antibacterial toilets as I had done in my previous job.

I was in the middle of sketching out a marketing framework when Elliott tapped me on the shoulder.

"I'm going to Donna's Diner for lunch. Do you want me to bring you back anything?"

"Oh, no thanks, I'm good. I brought something to munch on." I patted my satchel. "I think I should be finishing up here pretty soon."

"Ok, if you need to leave while I'm gone, just turn the lock and shut the door behind you. Make sure to pull hard. It's a bit warped. I've got my keys." He held up a compact set of keys. I doubted he had keys of unknown provenance like my own massive ring of keys.

I completed making notes inspired by the drawings and neatly stacked the papers in the file folder. I held the file in my hands and stared at the file cabinet. Two identical metal four-drawer filing cabinets stood next to each other, each with the locks popped out. Which drawer did he get this out of?

I pulled open a drawer at random. Judging by the plumbing and electrical company names printed on the file folders, these were subcontractor files. I opened another drawer.

At first glance, it appeared empty, but before I could shut it, I glimpsed a notebook wedged into the file cabinet that was similar to the one Perry had waved around the last time I'd been at the construction site. If Brenda's intel about a future housing development near my house was correct, maybe the Westen property was the other project Elliott had referred to. This notebook could hold more details about the future development and offer clues about my neighbor, Samuel Westen.

I cast a furtive glance at the door, but Elliott had only been gone for fifteen minutes. I had probably another twenty minutes minimum, maybe more considering how slow the service was at Donna's Diner. The notebook called out to me. It wouldn't hurt to take one little peek, right?

I removed it and sat down in front of the file cabinets. The first section was some sort of general ledger.

I wasn't an accountant, but it appeared the bank account being tracked was close to empty. I pulled out bank statements that were crammed into the front pocket of the ledger. Large monthly withdrawals had been made in cash every month. Someone had used a yellow highlighter on the withdrawals and scribbled a question mark next to them.

Something here wasn't right. Elliott had said to Perry, "We can't hold on much longer." What had he meant by that? Elliott had explained it away as regarding a new project, but was the condo project going bankrupt? What was the deal with the cash withdrawals? Although it was possible they were paying someone under the table for construction work, the regularity of the withdrawals seemed odd.

Elliott told me Perry had gone back East, but what if that wasn't true? Could Perry have stolen the money and skipped town? I flipped through the ledger pages to see how far back the withdrawals went. I was probably crazy to think anything was amiss. This whole Westen murder thing was really getting to my head. There couldn't possibly be this much crime happening in Ericksville at the same time.

Buzz, buzz. My phone vibrated. Shoot. It was Mikey's school. I carefully placed the notebook in the file cabinet as I answered the phone.

"Hi." I crossed my fingers hoping nothing major was wrong.

"Hello, Mrs. Andrews, it's Molly Devine from Busy Bees Preschool. I wanted to speak with you regarding Mikey's recent behavior."

I groaned and stood, opening the other drawers until I

found the correct one. I replaced the file folder with the artist's renderings and turned away from the cabinet.

"Is there a problem?" I paced the floor.

"Well, I don't know if I would call it a 'problem'. We prefer to think of something like this as an issue that we should work out with the child's parents."

"Ok, then. What seems to be the 'issue'?" I put as much emphasis on the word as she had.

"Mikey's been disrupting the class more than usual, and it's making it difficult for the other kids to learn. Today he even hit another child when that child tried to talk during circle time. Have there been any changes at home we should know about? Mikey's mentioned his father more than usual. Is his father still in the home?"

Great. Now Mikey's school thought that Adam and I were having marital problems. "No, Mrs. Devine," I said sweetly, "everything's fine at home. Mikey's father has been traveling more for work, and he probably misses him." I hoped Mikey wasn't in danger of being kicked out of school. Getting him into a new preschool in the middle of the school year would be no easy feat.

"I'm sorry to ask, but we need you to pick up Mikey within the hour. He's just too wound up to stay at school today."

"Ok, I'll be there in about ten minutes. I'll make sure to have a talk with Mikey tonight."

"That sounds like a good plan, Mrs. Andrews. Please let us know if there's anything we can do to help." She hung up.

I sat there, staring off into space for a moment. The job Gena had told me about sounded exciting, but if I was at work halfway across the country, who would pick Mikey up at school when he was in trouble or sick? Would a nanny care as much as I did? And how would me traveling so much affect my kids? Mikey was already getting in trouble, and I was only a mile away from preschool. I was pretty sure I wanted some type of job, but I had a sinking feeling that any job with significant travel wasn't in the cards for me. I shook my head to clear my thoughts. I'd call Gena later and let her know. At the moment, I needed to get to Mikey's school.

I hurriedly packed up the rest of my belongings and straightened the table I'd used as a desk. I locked up and pulled the door shut firmly behind me. I didn't know what was going on or why Elliott was being so secretive about development plans for Mr. Westen's land, but his construction project had just been set on fire. I wasn't going to be responsible for adding a burglary to his woes.

20

"So Mikey actually hit some kid for talking during circle time?" Desi munched away at a cookie I'd brought her from the café. I'd thought about bringing her brownies, too, but it seemed wrong in light of the Westen fiasco.

"From what I can get out of him, he didn't actually hit the other kid. His story is that the other kid was talking and getting him in trouble, so he nudged him to shut him up." I bit into a chocolate chip cookie of my own from the cookie tin. Yum. "I don't know what's true or not. I think having Adam gone so much is really affecting him though."

Desi's eyes turned downward. "It's hard to only have one parent at home. I hope Anthony is doing ok alone with Tomàs. Tomàs isn't used to having all the household responsibility, and Anthony can be a lot of work."

"Don't worry about Tomàs. When I picked Mikey up after the kids' sleepover, he was reading them a book, flipping pancakes, and unloading the dishwasher all at the same time. And not once did I see him flip a pancake into the dishwasher."

Desi laughed. "Yeah, he is a pretty amazing man. I'm lucky to have him." She rubbed her belly. "Baby's doing fine here, but I'm going nuts. I never thought I'd be jealous of someone getting to unload the dishwasher. So tell me what's going on with you. Did you start your new job?"

"My first day was yesterday. It's only a few hours a week. The owner wants me to create a website and other marketing materials for the condo project. Do you know Elliott Elkins? He's the owner of the development group. Actually it's named after him, Elkins Development Group."

"So he named a company after himself?" She shook her head with mirth. "I'm not surprised. Elliott has always been a little full of himself."

"Really? He seems like a nice guy. How long have you known him?"

"He is a nice guy—generally. Just don't mess with something he considers his property. If another guy tried to even look at Elliott's girl, they didn't take a second look, if you know what I mean. But he didn't have much to worry about." A dreamy look came over her face. "Is he still as hot as he was in high school? He was in the same class as Adam and when they were seniors, all of us freshman girls thought he was such a hunk."

"Desi! You're married. With 1.5 kids!"

"Married, not dead." Her eyes twinkled. "I've seen his name on things over the years but haven't run into him."

"Yes, Desi, he's still rather attractive. The fire at the condo complex hit him hard though. He and his business partner, Perry, have a lot of rebuilding to do."

"Perry Winston?"

"Yeah, I think so, why?"

"Perry was Elliott's best friend all through school. Not

quite as smart or attractive as Elliott, but always there for him. That's great that they went into business together.

"So how is my mom doing at the Boathouse without me?" Desi crunched into her third snickerdoodle cookie. "I see she's been busy baking."

"She seems a little stressed, but I've been helping out there too. We miss you."

"I miss being there and seeing everyone too." She quieted for a moment. "Hey, did you find anything out about the lease for the BeansTalk building?"

I squirmed in the hard plastic chair. What was I going to tell her? I should have known she'd ask. She narrowed her eyes at me.

"Jill, what are you not telling me? You're hiding something."

I squirmed again. "Nothing, this chair is making my butt go numb."

"C'mon, be honest. It's not going to kill me."

I looked pointedly at her midsection.

She sighed. "And not the baby either. I'm stronger than you all give me credit for. Spill."

"Ok, ok. I spoke with Anna, Samuel Westen's daughter. She found some paperwork that indicates the building might be under a sales contract already, but she was going to have someone look at it."

Desi lay back against her mound of pillows and folded her hands over her belly. "Ok, well, not what I wanted to hear, but at least it hasn't definitely been sold."

"Anna doesn't want to sell that property or anything else. Her mother was a member of one of Ericksville's founding families, and she's pretty passionate about preserving as much of the town history as possible. In fact, her mother was born in the house where Samuel Westen lived." I sat upright. "I didn't even get around to telling you about that. He planned to sell his house and land to Elliott for some massive housing development. Brenda told me all about it. But the weird thing is, Elliott denied everything when I asked him about the project."

"With everything going on with the fire at the condo building and the town's hatred of it, he'd be reluctant to discuss another controversial project." She looked thoughtful. "Your view and others' would be ruined if they built a whole bunch of houses there. But now because of Westen's death, the deal won't go through."

"Hey, what are you trying to say?" I teased. "Do you think I murdered him?"

"You'd have been standing in line with the rest of us," Desi joked back. "But if Anna wanted to preserve her mother's legacy, wouldn't she be pretty upset if she found out her father planned to subdivide the property her mother grew up on?"

"You have a point," I said slowly. "But I can't imagine her killing her own father—not that he was much of a father." I couldn't keep the secret about Elliott's parentage any longer. I told her all about Gwen and Benton's love affair and the resulting pregnancy.

"Does Elliott know?"

"No! And you can't tell him. Promise me?" I implored.

Desi feigned signing a cross over her heart. "I promise, but think of how hard that was for Elliott's mom. Tomàs and I have a tough time parenting Anthony, and there are two of us. She must have been a very strong woman to provide for her son as a single parent. Elliott is quite successful, so she must have done something right." We were both quiet for a moment. Adam was gone a lot, but she was right. I couldn't imagine not having his help with the kids.

"Time to take your vitals, Mrs. Torres." A nurse pushed a cart into the room and positioned it by the foot of the bed. I stood and placed my hand on Desi's.

"I'd better get going. I'll come visit again as soon as I can. Call me if I you need anything."

She smiled at me and squeezed my hand, but her smile wasn't as bright as when I'd entered the room. I never should have told her about the possible sale of the Beans-Talk Café building. Me and my big fat mouth and inability to lie well.

"What do you mean you 'accidentally' told Desi about the sale of her building?" Adam asked. I could almost see his icy death glare over the phone line.

"It was an accident. She asked about the lease, and I told her I didn't know. You know I don't lie well. Your sister saw right through me."

"Yes, I know my sister all too well. You didn't stand a chance with pit bull Desi. Once she gets her teeth clamped into something, there's no stopping her." He sighed. "Well, what's done is done. How are the kids?"

"Ella's fine, Mikey not so much." I relayed the details of the preschool 'issue.' "Adam, he misses you."

"I know. It's just a few more weeks." From years of marriage, I could tell Adam didn't even believe it anymore.

"I miss you," I said quietly. Tears formed in my eyes, and I swiped at them before I turned into a blubbering mess. "The house is so quiet at night, and I'm just tired of doing this alone all the time." How had Gwen Hanson managed all those years when it was only her and Elliott?

"How about we go out on a date when I get home Friday night? I'll have my parents watch the kids, and we can go out to that Italian place on Main Street we used to love," Adam said.

I eked out a smile. "I'd like that."

"Then it's a date," he said. "Honey, I've got to go, but I'm looking forward to seeing you on Friday. I love you."

"I love you too." I hung up the phone and leaned back in the recliner. I knew he was trying, but I wasn't going to count on him making it home in time for our dinner date.

It was already ten o'clock, but the cup of coffee I'd had after dinner wouldn't let me sleep any time soon. I puttered around downstairs washing dishes and folding laundry with the lights low. With those tasks complete, I settled down in my bed with the circus mystery and wrapped the covers around me tightly. Not even the mysterious monkey murderer could keep me awake with the sound of rain pattering gently on the roof.

Glass crashing downstairs woke me up way too early. I'd been in the middle of a dream involving Elliott Elkins, and not in a way Desi would approve of. Elliott had just finished chasing me down the street with a frying pan, intent on bashing my head with it.

Goldie barked frantically from downstairs in the living room. The alarm clock read 3:45 a.m. What had the cat broken now? I was sure I'd put the butter dish away in the fridge during my cleaning frenzy.

I pulled on my fuzzy purple bathrobe and slippers and

grabbed my cell phone off the bedside table just in case. I padded toward the stairs, ducking my head into the kids' rooms to check on them first. They continued to sleep soundly after all the racket. When I got to the foot of the stairs, it hit me that something wasn't right.

21

Cold air blew against my legs, and I pulled the bathrobe tighter. I flipped on the light. Goldie continued to bark at what I now could see was a broken windowpane. A glass pane directly above the doorknob of my patio door. I didn't see anyone in the house, but I wasn't sticking around to investigate further.

"Goldie. Come here." He bounded up the stairs after me and followed me from room to room as I grabbed a sleeping Mikey from his bed and laid him on the floor in Ella's room. I shoved a recliner against the door with more strength than I knew I possessed.

I had never in my life had to call 911 before, and now this was the second time I'd had to call in a week. Within five minutes, the 911 operator instructed me to go to the window. Searchlights strobed across my yard, and the police officer motioned to me to open the window.

"Mrs. Andrews," he shouted up at me. "We're going to enter the house now. Are you ok? Please stay put until we get to you."

"Yes, I'm fine." I slumped down against the wall where

the recliner used to sit. Goldie licked my hands and face. Miraculously, the kids continued to sleep.

After the police made their way upstairs, and I confirmed via a badge under the door that they were indeed real police, I pushed the chair aside and stepped out of the room, partially closing the door behind me.

"Did you find anything?" I was embarrassed to hear the shakiness in my voice.

"No, ma'am. The glass in the back door was broken and the door is unlocked, but there is no sign of an intruder in the house. I'd guess your dog scared them off before they could enter the house."

I patted Goldie's head. And Beth had said all our dog would do was lick an intruder. "So they didn't take anything?" I followed the police officer downstairs to the main living space.

"No. There's no sign that they were in the house at all. It may have been kids, but you were pretty lucky you had such a good guard dog here." He managed to say that with a straight face as Goldie nudged his open hand for a pet. "We'll take another look around outside, but we didn't find anything suspicious the first time through."

I started crying. The stress had finally gotten to me. I was glad Mikey wasn't awake to see me cry.

"Mrs. Andrews, do you have someone you can call? Maybe somewhere you can stay overnight?"

"Yes, my in-laws or my brother-in-law. He's a cop, but he's home alone with his son and I don't want to alarm them. I'll call my in-laws." Even with Beth and Lincoln's number on speed dial, my fingers tripped over the phone keys and it took several attempts before I successfully placed the call to them.

After getting over their initial shock of an early morning

phone call, Lincoln assured me we were welcome to stay with them and insisted on coming over to pick us up. I packed a few essentials and collapsed onto the living room sofa with Ella nearby in her bouncer. Mikey stirred a bit from where I'd moved him onto the living room recliner. That kid could sleep through anything. It was odd how I'd felt so secure in this same living room only six hours ago, and now I felt like I didn't even recognize the surroundings.

Outside, the policemen's lights flashed against the trees and bushes between our yard and Mr. Westen's house. Mikey would probably have made some comparison to light sabers and *Star Wars*, his new favorite movie.

Someone shouted outside and the lights descended on Westen's house. I got up to take a look out the window. The rain had stopped, but drops still fell off our upper deck and dripped onto the patio door, streaking the glass. I didn't even see the man on the patio until he'd opened the door.

I jumped backward reflexively. The policeman wiped off his feet on the doormat and looked up at me.

"Sorry, Mrs. Andrews. I wanted to come back and let you know what we found. It appears the house down the hill was also broken into tonight. Nothing seems to be stolen, so it probably was just kids messing around. We'll be done soon outside, but we'll send a patrol officer around every hour or so until morning. If we find anything else out, you'll receive a phone call." He left the house and walked down the path to his police car.

What was I going to do with this door? I'd need to call a locksmith and a glass place tomorrow. I swept up the glass and taped a piece of cardboard over the missing glass with duct tape. I stepped back to admire my work and then heard a sound at the front door.

Knock, knock.

Lincoln stood on the front porch, his fuzzy white hair sticking out in all directions. I stifled a grin. Normally rather vain about his remaining hair, he must not have taken the time to comb it before leaving. I opened the door and smiled weakly at him. Tears threatened to escape my eyes.

"Jill, are you ok?" His tall, well-built frame that was so much like Adam's was a comforting presence.

"Yeah, we're fine. The police think it was some kid, but I don't know. Mr. Westen's house was broken into too."

He closed the door firmly behind him and walked toward Mikey.

"I'll get Ella." I stooped to unbuckle my daughter from her bouncer, and her pink bunny rabbit caught my attention. It sat primly against the edge of an armchair next to the patio door.

Normally, I wouldn't be surprised by a toy in my living room, but the last time I remembered seeing the bunny was when Ella and I were at Mr. Westen's house, waiting for the plumber. How had it gotten into my house?

"What's wrong?" Lincoln asked, scanning my face.

I pointed at the bunny. "That wasn't there before."

He looked at me like I was crazy. "Are you sure? Maybe Mikey put it there. Or it dropped off the chair."

"No. I couldn't sleep earlier, so I picked up everything in the living room after the kids went to bed. It wasn't there."

"You've been under a lot of stress lately with Adam being gone and now this." He swept his hand through his hair and cleared his throat. "It seems unlikely that a burglar moved a toy."

The patterns on the sofa's throw pillows seemed to swim in front of me. I rubbed my eyes and sat down on the sofa. Had I put the bunny in the diaper bag at Mr. Westen's house and forgotten I'd done so? When my snooping had been interrupted by the plumber's arrival, I could have put the toy in the stroller or in the diaper bag.

"You're probably right." I didn't mention that the last time I remembered seeing the bunny was at Mr. Westen's house.

He drove us back to his house, where Beth helped get Mikey into the boys' room, and Ella and I settled into their guest bedroom. Mikey woke briefly after the car ride but fell asleep again quickly in the familiar bed at his grandparents' house. He'd be surprised when he woke up in the morning.

When I awoke, it took awhile to remember where I was. The sun streamed through the sheer white polka dot drapes, creating circles on the golden oak floors. What time was it? Why hadn't Ella woken me up? Her crib was empty. I sat up quickly and the sudden movement caused my head to throb. Ignoring the pain, I swung my legs out of bed and opened the door.

Mikey's laughter and his sister's full-bellied giggles floated up the stairwell. I closed the door and dressed quickly. Beth insisted on keeping the windows cracked at night for fresh air. While the house smelled great, I had to pull a sweatshirt over my head to ward off the chill.

Downstairs, Lincoln and my kids sat at the breakfast table. Judging by the quantity of syrup on Mikey's hands and face, he'd already devoured a stack of pancakes. Ella sat in her highchair, kicking her feet and gumming a piece of pancake while sucking down a bottle. It was all such a normal scene, you'd have thought we were there for a family brunch and not as a result of a late-night break-in.

"Do you want one?" Beth motioned to the stack of

pancakes while expertly tending to fresh ones still on the griddle. "There's bacon and muffins too. And coffee, of course."

I nodded and sat next to Mikey.

Lincoln selected a mug from the cabinet and filled it with coffee, setting it down in front of me.

"Mom, Mom! Do you see how much syrup I have? And Grandpa said I could have *three* pieces of bacon."

I smiled at Mikey over the top of my coffee cup. He was unfazed by waking up somewhere different than where he'd gone to bed the night before.

I slathered butter on a muffin and poured syrup over my stack of pancakes and reached for the bacon. A bite of the muffin reminded me of the source of Desi's baking skills. Yum. This was heaven. I contemplated milking the break-in and requesting to stay until Adam came home. In our house, toast and cereal were considered gourmet breakfasts during the week.

My face must have conveyed my desire to be a long-term house guest because Beth brought the remaining pancakes over to the table and said, "You're welcome to stay as long as you need to. I really think you should get an alarm system. This is the kind of thing that worries me about you being home alone with the kids. With Samuel Westen being murdered so close and the break-in at his house too, I really worry."

"Beth's right," Adam's dad said. "Ericksville isn't the same sleepy little town we grew up in. Crime has spread from the city, and you can't sleep with your doors unlocked anymore." His eyes drooped.

"My doors weren't unlocked!" I protested. "I double-checked them last night."

"I know, but my point is that it's gotten to the point

where an alarm system may be necessary. You live within walking distance of downtown and, with the public buses stopping down on Main Street now, there are so many vagrants looking for places to rob or sleep for the night. Look at the poor homeless guy who died in the condo fire. That never would have happened twenty years ago."

"Fine, I'll look into it." I glanced at the clock and did a double take. "I can't believe it's nine o'clock already. Mikey's going to be late for school, and I've got so much to do."

"Do you need me to take Ella today? I don't have any potential clients coming in today, and Tuesdays aren't popular for events." Beth daintily wiped her mouth with a cloth napkin.

"That would be great. I planned to stop in at the condo project to look at some of the plans, and then I'm taking a shift over at the BeansTalk. I figured I could bring Ella with me, but she'd probably be happier with you."

Beth cleaned off Ella's hands and face and picked her up. "Ella and Grandma are going to have fun at the mall today." She snuggled Ella close and gave her a kiss. "I just love having a little girl to spoil. Go ahead and leave Goldie here for the day too. Daisy loves having a friend to play with." She leaned down to pet the English bulldog pressed into the floor by her feet.

I was a little afraid of how many outfits Ella would come home with. But she was outgrowing her six-month clothes, so I'd skip the lecture about how many clothes one little girl could possible need.

"Sounds good. Mikey, c'mon, we need to get going."

"But Mom, I'm still eating," he whined. A piece of bacon hung out of his mouth, and he played idly with it.

"Mikey, we're going to be late. Let's go!" I silently counted to ten to calm my frustrations.

"No, Mom, I'm not done." He scowled at me.

Lincoln glared at his grandson, and Mikey slid off the chair and trudged down the hall to the bathroom, stomping his feet along the way. If this was what an almost-four-year-old was like, I wasn't looking forward to the teenage years.

"Thanks," I mouthed to my father-in-law. I gathered up my belongings and managed to get Mikey out to the front hallway looking somewhat clean. I had my keys in hand, ready to go out the door to my van, when I remembered I hadn't driven there.

"Lincoln, could you drive me home so I can get my car? Maybe we could drop off Mikey on the way?"

"Sure." He stuffed half a crumbling blueberry muffin in his mouth and grabbed his keys and jacket.

22

We pulled up to the parking lot of Busy Bees Preschool thirty minutes late.

"Is it ok to park here?" Lincoln pointed at the only parking space remaining in the lot. A neatly painted sign in front of the spot read, "Danielsen family only".

"Yeah, it'll only be for a few minutes. They offer that spot every year at the annual auction. Families bid crazy amounts of money for it. Shouldn't be a big deal to park there right now."

I got Mikey out of the car and caught a glimpse of a face peering through the window. By the time we had the door open, Nancy Davenport waited for us behind the front desk.

"Mikey, nice to see you. Your class is waiting for you. Please go on back," she said in a stern voice. I tried to slink out the door while she addressed my son.

"Jill, can we have a little chat please?" It seemed more like an order than a request.

"Sure," I said, pasting a smile onto my face. "What's going on? Is it my snack day?" I cast a glance at the snack calendar but didn't see Mikey's name.

"No. But please do remember to sign up. Some parents have had to provide more than one snack a month, but they shouldn't have to." She looked disapprovingly at me. "Actually, I wanted to remind you that the reserved parking spot out front isn't for all of our families to use for their convenience. The Danielsen family donated a large sum to the school for the sole use of that spot for the year."

"The parking lot was full and my father-in-law is still in the car." I gritted my teeth. I was going to have to start using the counting trick when dealing with Nancy too. "I didn't think it would be a big deal because school had already started. As soon as I leave, I'll have him move the car."

"Maybe next time, you should 'think' about getting Mikey to school on time. We are all concerned about his behavior lately. Children crave routine, you know." She folded her hands in front of her on the reception desk and smiled sweetly at me.

I didn't want to get into the details about the break-in. "I'll be sure to get him here on time tomorrow. Thank you for your concern, but I really need to leave now." The silent counting wasn't working and, if I stayed any longer, I'd have a YouTube video of my own. I spun around and opened the door. I pretended not to hear Nancy as she called out the door to me.

I yanked open the car door and threw myself into the seat. "Drive," I ordered as if I were a bank robber.

Lincoln raised an eyebrow. "Tough day at preschool drop-off?"

"You have no idea." We rode in silence to my house, where he stopped the car at the curb in front of the front door.

"Would you like me to come inside?"

"No, I'm fine." It seemed ridiculous to ask Lincoln to

check out the house. I stared at the house, then with trepidation, walked up the steps and unlocked the door. I wasn't sure I was ever going to shake the feeling that someone had violated my dream home. Maybe I did need an alarm system to feel better.

He turned off the car and stepped out. "Beth would never forgive me if I didn't walk you in." He zipped up his rain jacket and stepped over a puddle onto the front walk.

I slowly pushed open the door. Everything looked fine. I released the breath I didn't know I'd been holding. Fluffy ran to the door and milled around our feet. In all the commotion after the break-in, I'd forgotten her usual early morning feeding, a situation I quickly rectified.

Lincoln walked through the house. "Everything looks fine in here. The cardboard on the door is soggy, but it held."

I looked at him gratefully. "Thanks."

"No problem, let me know if there's anything we can do for you. And, Jill?" He paused. "Our house is always open for you and the kids."

I nodded and shut the door behind him. The house seemed eerily quiet without the kids and Goldie. The only sound was Fluffy crunching away on cat food in the laundry room.

I flipped on every light on the way to the living room and walked toward the patio door. Lincoln was right. The cardboard had held, but it wouldn't last much longer. I needed to get that locksmith and glass company out soon or our house would be flooded in the next bout of rain. I peered out the window. The low-hanging gray clouds threatened to dump rain on us at any time. Moving away from the window, I kicked something soft.

Ella's bunny.

How had it gotten there? Was Lincoln right and Mikey had placed it there? Had I not noticed? Last night, I'd been too bleary-eyed and disoriented to think clearly. Now, fortified with coffee and a hearty breakfast, I was sure the last time I'd seen it was at Mr. Westen's house.

Blood drained from my face. If the same person had broken into both the Westen house and our house, had they brought the toy here? What if it was the same person who killed Mr. Westen? Did they know I was conducting my own investigation?

I shivered, not from the draft coming through the cardboard, but from the realization that while my children and I slept upstairs, someone had entered my house and left my daughter's stuffed animal behind. I eyed the bunny and picked it up by one floppy ear. I walked quickly to the laundry room, scaring Fluffy in the process. I scavenged the dirty laundry, encased the bunny in the pillowcase I'd found, and threw it in the washing machine.

I wanted to throw the toy in the trash, but the bunny had the power to make Ella smile when she was cranky. I wasn't going to let the intruder take any more happiness away from my family, and I refused to let it frighten me away from finding out who really killed Mr. Westen. For Desi's and the baby's sake, the real murderer needed to be found ASAP, and I would do anything I could to make that happen.

23

My first call of the day was to a locksmith and glass repair company. Then, I phoned an alarm system company. I scheduled installation of a fancy system with all the bells and whistles for the next day. I took a quick shower, changed into work clothes and hopped into my car. I wasn't due at the BeansTalk until one o'clock, but I needed to do some more research on the condo project for the marketing plan I'd started.

The door to Elkins Development Group was ajar, and I pushed it in without knocking. Elliott sat at his desk, fiddling with a pair of black-rimmed glasses. He didn't look up when I entered.

"Elliott?" I knocked on the door to alert him to my presence. He looked up. If possible, he looked even worse than when I'd seen him the day before. His hair hung in greasy strands and his tan was fading fast.

"Jill, hi," he said. "What can I do for you?" He sounded somewhat irritated to see me, but he smiled broadly.

"I need to take a look at those architectural designs

again. I've got an idea to promote the condos, but I have to check some things first."

"Sure, go ahead." He motioned to the file cabinets. "They're in the drawers."

I put down my bag next to the small side desk I'd used last time. Would the ledgers still be there? I started to open the bottom drawer where I'd seen the notebook, but I only had it open a crack when Elliott cut in.

"In the third drawer down."

"Oh, thanks. So many drawers, I forgot where they were."

I'd seen enough of the drawer to know the notebook was no longer there. I pulled open the correct drawer and withdrew the documents I needed, bringing them over to my workspace.

Elliott cleared his throat and looked at the clock on the wall and then at me, as if deciding what to do. "Jill, I've got to run an errand. Are you ok here alone?"

I nodded.

"My cell phone is on the fritz, and I'm expecting a phone call here. Would you mind answering the phone while I'm gone?" Elliott asked.

"No problem." I smiled in what I hoped was a confident manner.

Was I ok alone in here? Ha! Mikey's school had interrupted me last time, and I felt giddy at the chance to snoop more. Elliott's lies about the Westen property worried me. I wanted to know the truth before a whole bunch of new cottage homes popped up on the hillside below my house.

Elliott left and I quickly got to work. Unfortunately, the file cabinets yielded nothing useful. A quick search of Elliott's desk produced a business card for Derek Kim, CPA.

Had Elliott brought the company records to his accountant for safekeeping?

Ring! Ring!

The phone startled me. What was it with phone calls interrupting me here? It took me a few seconds to realize it was the desk phone ringing.

"Elkins Development Group," I said professionally. "How may I help you?"

A worried female voice came over the line. "Is Perry there?"

"No, I'm sorry, ma'am. Perry is out of town."

"Out of town? He was supposed to be here for our hearing, but he never showed up. That bastard." The worry had turned to anger.

"I'm sorry, I don't know the details. If I could get your name and number, I can leave a message for him to call you back."

"Never mind." She hung up.

I set the receiver down and sat down at the desk. Was that Perry's ex-wife? If he hadn't flown to Baltimore, where was he?

24

Nobody else called while Elliott was grabbing lunch. When he returned, I left and drove to the BeansTalk on autopilot, my brain spinning like a washing machine on turbo speed. Had Perry skipped town after draining the condo project's bank accounts? I parked in the side lot of the BeansTalk. Underneath my feet, the cracked pavement still held remnants of the rain storm from the night before. A fog hung over the Sound, blocking the view of Willowby Island. I felt like I was in the middle of a cloud.

The bells jingled as I opened the door of the café. Mandy glanced up from the counter and waved.

"Not much going on today?" I nodded at the open textbook on the counter.

"Nope, it's been pretty slow. It's ok to study when we're slow, right? Desi said it was fine, and I have a math test tomorrow," Mandy said quickly. "All the dishes are washed and the tables are cleaned off."

"No worries, it looks great in here. Thanks for taking the extra shift. You can go now—I'm covering until close." I shivered and pulled my sweater closer. “Why is it so cold in here?” When I’d come to visit Desi before, the BeansTalk had always been a warm, cozy, and inviting place to have a cup of coffee and a piece of cake. I’d assumed the atmosphere was due to the cheerful yellow walls and children’s artwork up on the walls. Now, I wondered if Desi’s energetic presence had created the impression of warmth.

“I didn’t turn the heater on because it was supposed to warm up this afternoon, and I didn’t want it to get too hot with the ovens going,” Mandy said.

With air-conditioning a luxury in our moderate climate, we hoarded the morning chill as a means of keeping our buildings temperate.

“If that fog ever lifts, it should warm up a bit,” I said. I didn’t think the lack of heat was the only reason the atmosphere felt off. The BeansTalk was Desi’s passion, and her enthusiasm for the business was a big reason for the usual steady stream of business.

Mandy took off the apron she wore over her street clothes, picked up a stack of textbooks, and flung a backpack over her arm.

“Thanks, Mrs. A. Let me know if you need me to work any other shifts. After this math final, I’m pretty much clear for the week.” She scurried out the door.

I took a BeansTalk apron from a neatly folded pile and smoothed it over my body, tying it tightly at the waist. My sneakers squeaked on the hardwood floors as I made a pass through the room. Mandy was right, everything looked great. I hoped that didn’t mean business had been slow. I inhaled the cinnamon- and espresso-scented air and settled down on the stool Mandy had previously occupied. My stomach translated the deliciously scented air into hunger pangs, even though I’d eaten recently.

After ten minutes had passed without any customers, I got up to stretch and walked to the back room. Here, too, everything was in order. Although the BeansTalk sold freshly baked goods made in the Boathouse's full kitchen, Desi had shelves of stable goodies as well. Neat rows of tins on one wall contained biscotti, wrapped chocolates, swizzle sticks, and sugar packets. Airtight glass jars of coffee beans and tea bags lined the other wall.

The brightly painted yellow walls in Desi's office beckoned. I stood in the doorway, taking in the view beyond the only window in the customer-restricted area of the store. The Ericksville Lighthouse loomed above, the waves of the Sound lapping at the beach behind it. The fog had cleared slightly, and the cliffs of Willowby Island provided the perfect frame for the white lighthouse tower. It would be a shame for her to lose the lease on this building.

Desi's desktop computer was perched on one corner of the small desk with paperwork stacked neatly along the edges. Beth had been here. Although Desi was an amazing small business owner, organization was not her strong suit. A pill bottle near the corner of the monitor caught my eye. I leaned over and picked it up. Digal? The medicine sounded familiar. I turned the bottle over in my hands to read the patient's name. My heart dropped into my shoes.

The pills belonged to Beth. I did a quick internet search for the medicine and found it was prescribed for heart problems.

Was Beth sick? I couldn't imagine anything happening to her, and she always seemed to have so much energy. I suddenly realized that while I never thought of Adam's parents as aging, they were getting into their late sixties. I felt a pang of guilt thinking about how often I left Mikey and his hyperactive behavior with Beth and Lincoln. Beth claimed to love having her grandson visit, but now I worried that it was too much for her.

She had thrown out hints that she wanted to take things easier and decrease her responsibilities at the Boathouse. Desi was being groomed to take over marketing at the Boathouse, but with her recent hospital incarceration, that was put on hold indefinitely. Now, Beth had her daughter's health, the police investigation, and running the BeansTalk added to her plate. She lived for her family and would do anything for them, but maybe it was too much. I needed to have Adam talk with his mother. If he was ever home long enough to do so, that was.

The doorbell jingled, alerting me to the presence of a customer. I sprinted to the front of the shop and greeted them with a huge smile. The harried mother of a sullen elementary school-aged boy and a cherubic toddler asked for a quadruple espresso and three brownies. She grabbed for the drink as soon as I pulled the shots and took a long swig before smiling gratefully at me.

The boy plopped down at a table and pulled out a Nintendo DS, defiantly shoving headphones over his ears. The little girl went from cherubic to devilish in a flash and raced to the back of the café, screaming at the top of her lungs as she pushed chairs aside. Now I understood the quadruple shot drink. The mom took off after her offspring and managed to downgrade the tornado to a Category 2 storm.

A mom's work was never done. An image of Beth came to mind. I returned to Desi's office and picked up the orange bottle of pills.

I'd been so wrapped up in disbelief that my seemingly healthy mother-in-law took heart medicine that it took me awhile to remember where I'd heard the name of the medicine before.

Beth Andrews had a prescription for the same drug that had poisoned Samuel Westen. I set the bottle down on the desk and pushed it away as though it had suddenly become radioactive.

The door bells jingled again and I went out to greet the incoming customer, but my mind wasn't on business. When had Beth left the prescription bottle here? Before Mr. Westen's murder? Did Desi have access to it? Tomàs had said the brownies showed no trace of the drug, which made sense since the brownies were intended for Adam and not Mr. Westen. But Desi freely admitted she had made a visit to Mr. Westen after the town council meeting, and she could have drugged him at that time. She claimed she'd only made it as far as his front porch, but anyone who'd seen her there might think differently. As far as I knew, the wrath of Desi's temper only extended to pen throwing, but had Mr. Westen pushed her over the edge?

"Excuse me?" A man tapped his fingers on the counter. "I'd like to order."

I smiled and apologized for ignoring him. I handed him his triple shot, soy vanilla latte and watched as he left the café.

It hadn't occurred to me before, but Beth had a motive in Samuel Westen's murder. Her daughter was about to be hurt by Westen and, as a mother myself, I knew protecting her children was a top priority. But would she go as far as murder to save her daughter's business?

I was spinning rapidly down a rabbit hole that didn't have a pleasant end. The acid from the coffee I had drunk earlier burned a hole in my stomach. Now that I knew about

Beth's prescription, I wasn't sure I could forget about it. Samuel Westen's murderer needed to be found, and fast.

~

At five o'clock, I locked up the BeansTalk and got into my car. The warm day the weatherman had promised had never materialized, and my car felt chilly. I'd planned to have dinner with Beth and Lincoln, but I wasn't due there until later, and they had picked up Mikey and Anthony already. On impulse, I drove to the southern part of town.

I pulled up in front of an office complex buried in the trees. A discreet sign in front of the furthest office from the parking lot entrance said "Derek Kim, CPA." Two cars were parked directly in front of the door. As I watched the door, a gust of wind blew a yellow McDonald's hamburger wrapper across the parking lot. I'd had enough of spring. In my opinion, summer couldn't come fast enough.

Inside the CPA's office, a woman stood with her back to the glass door, her hand on the door handle as she spoke with someone I couldn't see. When she pushed the door open and reached down for her sunglasses, I realized it was Anna Westen. I shouldn't have been surprised since she'd mentioned visiting her father's accountant, but I hadn't realized Samuel Westen had used the same accountant as the Elkins Development Group. I got out of the car and walked toward her.

Anna brushed past me as though she didn't see me.

"Anna!" I called out. "Hi."

She turned and lowered her sunglasses. In doing so, she lost her grip on a handful of paperwork. A breeze caught the papers and scattered them around the parking lot. She bent to pick up the nearest papers, and I ran toward one that had flown to the other side of my car. Before handing it back to her, I glanced at the document, which bore the name Ericksville Properties. Hmm. Must have been one of her father's companies.

"Thank you for catching those. It's nice to see you." She smiled and then looked confused. "I didn't expect to see you here. Small towns are full of surprises."

I had my excuse at the ready. "My sister-in-law is looking for a new accountant for the BeansTalk, so I'm interviewing CPAs for her. How do you like Derek Kim?"

"I don't really know him. My father transferred his business to Derek right before he died." Anna checked her watch. "I've got to go. I'm late to pick up my son from practice. I really appreciate your help with my father's house." She waved goodbye to me and then scurried to her car. I turned to look at the CPA office.

Empty flowerbeds bordered the utilitarian concrete walkway. I pulled on the handle to open the door. Inside, a rubber welcome mat covered fraying Berber carpet. Any profits from the business weren't going back into the décor. It was in sharp contrast to the high class décor of Elkins Development Group, even after the recent fire. A receptionist desk was pressed against a wall, surrounded by filing cabinets, but I didn't see anyone in the building. Anna had been talking with someone, so they must have been in another room.

"Hello?" I called.

"Just a minute." A man's voice drifted down from a stairway near the door I hadn't noticed before. "I'll be right with you."

After a few minutes, a middle-aged Asian man walked down the stairs.

"Hi, I'm Derek Kim. And you are?"

"Jill Andrews." I stuck out my hand. "Nice to meet you." He shook my hand limply.

"What can I do for you today?" he asked.

"I'm helping my sister-in-law search for a new accountant for her café, and I hoped to ask you a few questions today. I'm sorry to drop in so late. Is this time ok?"

Derek checked an expensive-looking watch that coordinated perfectly with his well-made gray suit. Now I knew where he spent his money.

"Now is fine. I'm not usually in this late, but I had a client meeting."

"Actually, I saw your client leave. Anna Westen's father was a neighbor of mine. Was he your client? I know it's been difficult for her to get his finances in order. "

Derek's oily grin slipped for a moment but was quickly recovered. "I'm sorry, I can't comment on my clients. Confidentiality and all. I'm sure you understand." His smile was still pleasant, but his eyes had turned to steel. "Let's go in my office where we'll be more comfortable."

He guided me into a sparsely furnished office. No fancy decanters or water pitchers for him. His desk held little more than a computer. A round cut glass container of potpourri surprised me.

"What a beautiful bowl."

Derek's smile softened into something more real as he gazed at the bowl. "My niece thought I needed something nice in here. I have to admit it does smell pretty good." He looked up at me. "What can I tell you about my practice here? I specialize in financial statements, bookkeeping, and taxes for small businesses."

"My sister-in-law is looking for someone to take over the bookkeeping for her business. She's not much on numbers. Her mother is currently doing the bookkeeping, but she's overwhelmed with a business of her own. They've been doing everything on paper but might be interested in setting up a computer accounting system."

"Sure. I'd be happy to help. Let me tell you about my fees." He withdrew a piece of paper from a desk drawer and explained to me the intricacies of his fee schedule. I leaned in to listen more intently before I remembered why I was really there. How was I going to get into the CPA's file cabinets to see the Elkins Development Group books? Was their business really going bankrupt?

Achoo! A sneeze caught me unaware, and I sat back abruptly.

"Are you alright?" Derek asked.

"Yes, I'm fine." I sneezed again. Some scents really bothered me, and I must have been mildly allergic to the potpourri. Inspiration struck and I threw myself into a coughing fit.

"Ms. Andrews—are you ok?"

"It's the potpourri. I must have inhaled it or something."

"Is there anything I can do? Maybe get you something to drink?" He whisked the cut-glass bowl away, and I saw visions of a potential lawsuit flood his mind.

"A cup of tea would be wonderful." I coughed more for emphasis. "It would really help my throat. It feels a bit inflamed."

"I'll be right back. I think I have some upstairs in the kitchenette." Derek rushed away and sprinted up the stairs, taking them two at a time. If I wanted a glimpse of the contents of those file cabinets, this was my chance.

I heard rummaging around upstairs, so I tiptoed out of the room and found the file cabinet marked "E." Bingo. Elkins Development Group.

The hanging file contained the ledger I'd seen at the

EDG office, bank statements, and the partnership agreement. I quickly noted Elliott was listed as the president and Perry was the vice-president. The ledgers and bank statements confirmed my suspicion that EDG was almost bankrupt. They appeared to have made weekly payments of $9,999 each to Ericksville Properties for the last year. Why would EDG pay that much on a weekly basis for so long? I remembered from my job as a bank teller in college that banks must report any transaction over ten thousand dollars. The amount seemed suspicious, and Ericksville Properties sounded familiar. I stuffed the EDG documents back into the hanging file and replaced the folder back in the file cabinet—right in front of the file for Ericksville Properties.

Upstairs, the microwave dinged. Derek would return soon. I thumbed through the Ericksville Properties bank statements and saw the incoming weekly payments that matched the outgoing payments from EDG. What was Ericksville Properties, and why were they receiving large sums of money?

I opened the Ericksville Properties folder and read through the incorporation papers. My eyes widened. Anna Westen was listed as the company owner. I scanned through the other legal documents. Loopy A's and W's stood out prominently in girlish handwriting. Anna had signed every document. All along I'd thought Samuel Westen had been Derek Kim's client. Had I been wrong?

Footsteps sounded on the stairwell. I shoved the folder back into the file cabinet and pushed the drawer shut without a sound. I tiptoed quickly back to the office and had just sat down when Derek Kim rounded the corner of the stairs. I coughed lightly for good measure as I turned to him. As he passed the file cabinets, he bent to pick up a piece of paper from the floor, carefully balancing the hot cup of tea in one hand. Had the paper been there before I'd dug through the files? A chill ran down my spine. Had I dropped it? Derek looked puzzled and then his face turned impassive as he placed the paper on top of the file cabinet. He smiled at me as he entered the room.

"Here you go, Mrs. Andrews." He handed me the cup of tea. I dunked the string of the Red Rose tea bag a few times and took a sip.

"Thank you so much. This helps a lot." I drank more to sell my act. "I'm not usually quite so allergic to potpourri, but I must have inhaled some when I leaned in to view the fee list." Did he know I'd been in the file cabinet? I peered at him over the edge of my cup, but his face didn't reveal any suspicion.

"Yes, we were reviewing the fee list, weren't we?" He smoothly took out the list and pushed it in front of me again. "As you can see, my fees are quite reasonable, and I can help you with any accounting needs from bookkeeping to taxes. I'm a full-service accountant."

Did full-service include helping his clients hide evidence of blackmail? I was suddenly all too aware of the sliding glass door that overlooked a small pond behind the isolated office building. When I'd arrived, there had been no other cars in the parking lot except mine, Anna's, and the BMW I assumed belonged to Derek.

I set the mug of tea down on the desk and pointedly glanced at the brass clock behind his desk. "Oh, I've got to pick up my kids soon. Thank you so much for telling me about your services. I'll be sure to let my sister-in-law know." I rushed out of the office and didn't look back until I was safely in my car.

Derek ran outside after me.

"Mrs. Andrews!" He appeared at the driver's side window.

"Yes?" My voice cracked on the word, and I thought my heart would jump out of my chest.

"You forgot your jacket." He held up the lightweight khaki jacket I'd left on a chair in his office when I made my hasty retreat. I rolled the window down as little as possible to allow room for the jacket. He stuffed it through the opening.

"Thank you. I've got to go." I closed the car window. Derek retreated to the sidewalk and fiddled with the light outside the door, gazing at me with narrowed eyes. I backed out of the spot and hightailed it out of the parking lot faster than a teenager doing donuts.

Did Derek Kim know anything about what I assumed were blackmail payments? And how was Anna involved with all of this? I felt like an idiot for believing her innocent estranged daughter routine. She was in this deeper than she'd admitted. With her job as a paralegal, she probably knew exactly how to set up a shell company and hide evidence of blackmail. I felt as though I were in a fog. I'd become complacent living in a small town and seeing the best in everyone.

A squirrel ran out in front of me, and I slammed on my brakes. When I resumed a normal driving speed, the adrenaline from the abrupt stop had cleared my mind. I didn't know whether or not Anna was involved with any of this, or even if there was blackmail. But someone had killed Mr. Westen, and I still didn't know why. I decided that the next opportunity I had, I would ask Anna about her involvement with Ericksville Properties. For all I knew, there was a reasonable explanation for all of it.

25

After dinner at the in-laws', I bustled the two kids and the dog into the minivan and drove home. The discovery of the ownership of Ericksville Properties hung heavily on my mind. I wanted to know the truth about the mysterious transactions revealed by the bank statements.

The chance to talk with Anna came sooner than I'd imagined. When I pulled into my driveway, I saw there was a white envelope propped up on the front door welcome mat.

I drove into the garage and watched the door close completely behind me before getting the kids out of the car. When I opened the door to the house, Goldie ran past me and he and Fluffy almost bowled us over begging for food. We waded through a teeming sea of fur. Ella was still asleep in her carrier, and I set it down by the front door. Mikey followed me.

"Honey, can you please go play with your puzzles in the living room?" I asked him.

He frowned at me. "But Mom, I want to go with you."

"Mikey, go to the living room. Now." My patience had

worn thin. I wanted to know what was in the envelope. I wasn't expecting any packages, and this didn't look like it had been dropped off by FedEx or UPS. Mikey pouted but complied with my request.

I unlocked the front door, opened it a crack, and scanned the front yard for anything suspicious. The break-in had me spooked. Seeing nothing out of the ordinary, I stepped out onto the front porch, and gently pulled the door closed behind me.

The white envelope had slid down flat on the rubber mat. I picked it up. It appeared to be an ordinary greeting card, with the trademark Hallmark gold seal on the back. My name was printed neatly on the front.

Leaning against the closed door, I slid my forefinger along the back of the envelope to break the seal. I pulled out a greeting card imprinted with the image of a purple flower. Something fell out of the card and clattered down on the concrete porch. I picked up the plastic rectangle that had dropped out, opened the greeting card, and read the message.

"Thank you so much for your help with my father's house. Please accept this one hundred dollar gift card as a token of my appreciation." The scrawled signature was difficult to make out, but I deciphered it as Anna Westen's.

I turned over the credit card–shaped piece of plastic and saw the blue wave logo for Serenity Spa, a well-respected hair salon and spa overlooking the water in downtown Ericksville. A few friends had raved about the spa over the years, and I'd secretly wanted to visit, but I couldn't justify spending the money. It was an incredibly generous gift. Anyone who gifts someone with two small children a ticket to a child-free oasis couldn't be that bad. I was determined to find out how Anna was involved with Ericksville Properties.

I opened the front door a crack and peeked into the house. Ella was still sleeping soundly in her carrier, and I could hear Mikey playing with his Jake and the Never Land Pirates action figures in the living room. I eased the door closed again and pulled out my cell phone to call Anna.

"Hello?"

"Hi, Anna? It's Jill Andrews."

"Hi Jill."

"I wanted to call and thank you for the gift card. I've heard great things about the Serenity Spa. I was excited to see the card, but I almost didn't know who it was from. Your signature is barely legible!"

Anna's laugh echoed over the phone line. "My son tells me all the time I should have been a doctor, my handwriting is so bad. That's why I print everything. I think it's years of signing my name as witness to so many legal documents at work. Anyways, I'm so glad you liked it. I figured you could use some adult time, and you've been such a big help to me with my father's house."

"Do I look that frazzled?" I kept my tone light so she'd know I was teasing.

"No, definitely not. When I saw you at the CPA office this evening I remembered I wanted to get you something to thank you," Anna said. I was surprised she mentioned the CPA office since she had so studiously tried to avoid me there.

"You seemed rather distracted there. It must be difficult tracking down all your father's assets."

"It's definitely been a challenge." Anna sighed. "My father recently transferred his accounting to Derek Kim, so even Derek isn't completely sure of my father's whole financial picture."

"Did he have a lot of business holdings? For some reason, I thought he only had the few rentals in town. Then again, I didn't know him well." My approach was awkward, but I couldn't think of a good way to transition the subject of conversation to Ericksville Properties. I needn't have worried about changing the topic.

Anna was quiet for a few seconds, and then her voice became steely. "My father had several business entities I didn't know about. And apparently I'm the president of one of them." Her calm broke and she snuffled a little into the phone before I heard the telltale sound of a nose being blown into a Kleenex.

"Anna, what do you mean you're the president?"

"What I mean is that bastard forged my signature to a whole slew of legal documents. I'm now the president and owner of a property group with holdings across the county."

"He forged your signature? Isn't that illegal?" I asked. "You had no idea this company existed?"

"Nope." She blew her nose again. "Of course, I knew he owned some properties in town but not to this extent. I've been a millionaire all these years and I didn't even know it." She laughed ironically. "I should have been going on trips to Bermuda myself instead of faxing documents to clients on vacation there."

"But why did he forge your signature?"

"I don't know. Probably to avoid estate taxes or something. My father would do anything to make or save a buck."

None of this made sense. Was Anna telling the truth? Did she not know about Ericksville Properties?

"Oh, I wanted to tell you. I just found out that the sale of the BeansTalk property never went through. Desi doesn't need to worry about her café for a long while as I have no intention of selling the building."

Tears sprung to my eyes. "That's some of the best news I've heard all week. It will mean the world to Desi. Thanks, Anna."

From inside the house, Ella cried. A minute later, Mikey opened the door and announced his sister was awake. It was late, and I needed to feed Ella a bottle and get both kids to bed.

"Anna, I'm so sorry, but I've got to go. If you want, maybe we can talk about this later? That does seem odd about the company." Ella's screams had risen to a crescendo, and I rushed to get off the phone. "Thanks again for letting me know about the café building sale not going through and the gift. I'm looking forward to using it."

"Don't worry about it. I'm sure it will work out. Go, I can hear the baby crying. Thanks again for being a good neighbor... and friend." She hung up the phone.

I thought about calling Desi with the good news, but I worried about waking her up. I'd tell her the next day. I got the kids into bed with minimal resistance from Mikey and sat down to relax on the living room couch. I picked up the envelope and withdrew the gift card, flipping it between my fingers. This would be a nice treat with everything that had been going on.

Somehow, though, it felt tainted. I still wasn't sure whether to believe Anna's innocence.

I opened the card again to read Anna's kind message. My eyes were drawn to the bottom of the card. The boldly scrawled signature was not the same bubbly signature as the one I'd seen at Derek Kim's office on all the paperwork for Ericksville Properties.

Anna had told me the truth about the forged signatures.

But if Anna didn't know about the monthly payments being deposited into the account from Elkins Development Group, her father must have been responsible for what I hypothesized were bribes. Who was bribing Samuel Westen and why?

26

Thursday morning, after I dropped Mikey and Anthony off at preschool, I drove to the Boathouse to get the baked goods for the BeansTalk Café.

The Boathouse was quiet, and I found Beth poring over files in her office. She heard me approach, looked up, and smiled at me.

"Good morning," she said with more enthusiasm than I could muster at nine a.m. "I've got everything in the kitchen, ready to go." She jumped up from her desk and led the way to the kitchen. I lugged Ella in her car seat through the Boathouse's long hallway.

Boxes of scones, brownies, and oatmeal raisin cookies lined the kitchen island's counters. My eyes widened.

"Whoa," I said. Beth must have stayed up all night baking.

"I started at four o'clock this morning," she said, as if reading my mind.

I stared at her. The energy levels she had at her age put mine to shame. How did she do everything she did? I remembered the heart medication I'd found. Beth wasn't quite the robot I sometimes thought her to be.

"This should be enough for today and tomorrow at the Café." She folded the lids closed on the boxes and stacked them together. "I can make more on Saturday morning, before the afternoon wedding prep begins."

"Do you need help?" I felt horribly guilty. If Beth was sick, she shouldn't be working this hard.

She waved her hand. "Nope, I'm good."

I must have had a concerned expression on my face because she said, "What? Why do you look so worried?"

"I don't want to overwork you." I leaned against the counter.

"*Pshaw*. I've been working long hours since I was a teenager. I'm not slowing down anytime soon." Beth scanned my face. "What's going on?"

I bit my lip. Should I say something about the pills?

She put her hands on her hips. "Did one of my kids say something about me?"

"No, no." I sighed. "I found a bottle of your pills on Desi's desk at the Café."

"Oh," Beth said.

"Is it something we should be worried about? You work way too hard," I said. I looked down at Ella in her car seat carrier. She blew bubbles at me. I felt worse thinking about how many times I'd left the kids with Beth to babysit. Even if she wanted to do everything, she needed time to rest.

"No, it's nothing."

"Beth, they're heart pills. I looked them up. It's not nothing."

"My doctor wanted me to take them because I've had some chest pain. It's just anxiety, but he was worried." She smiled at me. "Honestly, don't worry, I'm fine."

"With Desi and everything, I can imagine you'd be under a lot of stress." I watched her face.

Beth's expression fell, but she quickly recovered. "I have faith that Desi and the baby will be just fine. I'm sure the police will clear her soon, and everything will work out."

"But what if it doesn't?" I asked. "It seems like they're stuck on her as a suspect."

"She didn't kill Samuel Westen."

"I know, but they haven't found a better suspect," I said. "Beth, he was poisoned with the same medication that you take."

"What? You think I killed him?" She laughed and then took a closer look at me. "You're kidding, right?"

My face burned. I had considered the possibility. "No, of course I don't think you killed him. But Desi had access to your pills. What if the police find out?"

"There's no reason that they would," Beth said. "The pills weren't at the café when the police went through the building. They're safely in my medicine cabinet now. Desi had nothing to do with Sam Westen's death."

"Ok, I know." I sagged against the counter. "Beth, I'm getting really worried about her. She's trying so hard to not let this bother her, but I can tell she's worried. Oh, but I heard from Anna Westen that the café building won't be sold. At least something is going our way."

Beth hugged me. "Honey, that's great news. But there's nothing we can do about the police investigation. I've asked around about Sam Westen's enemies but haven't come up with anything. Ultimately, we have to let the police figure out who really killed him."

I nodded. "I know. Thanks. Can you watch Ella while I run these out to the car?" Beth was already on the floor talking to her granddaughter and nodded in agreement.

I picked up the stack of baked goods and left Beth in the Boathouse's kitchen. After getting the pastries safely into the back of my minivan, I returned to get Ella. Beth looked sad to have her leave, and I promised I'd bring her back soon. I may have agreed with Beth that the police were ultimately responsible for finding the real killer, but that didn't mean I was going to stop my own investigation.

When I got home, a vase of flowers awaited me on the porch—red roses interspersed with delicate baby's breath, my favorite. I knelt to pick up the card. *Looking forward to our date tomorrow night. I love you. –Adam.* My eyes teared up. Adam might not always be physically there for me, but I always knew he loved me. And after what I'd gone through in the last two weeks, the reminder of his love meant the world. I brought Ella's carrier and the vase inside and snuggled up on the couch with the flowers for awhile, inhaling their heavenly scent and dreaming of happier times in the future.

The next afternoon, I pulled my minivan into an approved parking spot at the Busy Bees Preschool. Before launching myself into the chaos of forty preschoolers, I turned off the ignition and leaned back against the headrest, drawing the strength I knew I'd need to get through preschool pickup. I needed to get in, get the kids, and deliver them to my in-laws. I had three hours until my dinner date with Adam, so even with some primping time, I should have more than enough time to get ready. Especially if Nancy Davenport wasn't around.

I opened my eyes and scanned the parking lot. Across the parking lot was another minivan, this one with five stick figure people and a stick dog on the back window. Nancy was here, probably lying in wait to shove the gerbils at me. In an immature moment, I stuck my tongue out at her perfect little stick family.

As I walked past the back window, I could see Nancy's white-blonde hair over the top of the reading circle chair. With any luck, she'd be so engrossed in reading to the kids that she wouldn't notice me signing Mikey and Anthony out of school. I coaxed the door open and signed them out with a minimum of noise.

On the wall opposite the desk, the familiar pumpkin-colored auction committee flyer stuck out in a sea of other notifications. I scanned the list of important dates, and my heart dropped into my stomach. The first meeting was tonight. Brain cells churned as I walked to the back classroom to get the kids. Ok, if I hurry, I should be able to make the meeting at six p.m. and cut out a little early to meet Adam at seven. The Italian restaurant was only a block away from the school. I'd just need to get ready for our date before I left for the auction committee meeting.

Someone tapped me on the back. I spun around without thinking.

"Jill, nice to see you." Nancy's smile was as sweet as saccharine and just as fake.

"Hi." I couldn't fake a return greeting, so I settled for a half smile. She maneuvered around so I was forced to turn toward the class gerbils, racing around their wheel. I still couldn't understand why sane people wanted to keep rodents as pets. Nancy gestured at the gerbils.

"I'm glad you've decided to help out with the classroom pets. It's so important that all the families have a chance to be responsible for them. I know other parents have already gone above and beyond their duties, and it's so nice to see you stepping up." Nancy reached into the magazine holder next to the gerbil cage and withdrew a small pamphlet entitled "How to Care for a Gerbil."

She shoved it at me, and I took it automatically, still not saying a word for fear of what I'd say.

"I'll go get their travel carrier." She brushed past me to enter the storage room.

"Mom." Small hands tugged at the hem of my shirt.

"Mikey!" I leaned down to hug him. "I'm so glad to see you." I ruffled Anthony's hair. "And you too, of course."

"Mom, we get to take Sugar and Spice home with us for the weekend." Mikey looked so excited at the possibility that I tried to convince myself that having vermin in my house was no big deal. They were actually kind of cute, right? But the more I looked at their beady little eyes and twitching tails, I felt like I was going to hyperventilate.

"You know, I think we're actually signed up to do it sometime next month."

"But Mom, Miss Nancy said I got them this week." Mikey pouted.

"Well, I just talked with her and she left without giving them to me, so I think there was some sort of mix-up. I'll talk with her next week about it." I crossed my fingers behind my back. It wasn't too much of a lie, and it was a mix-up. I certainly had never promised to take the gerbils home with me. I pulled the two of them out the door to the car as quickly as I could without tripping them.

"How's my mom doing? And my baby sister?" Anthony asked as I belted him into his car seat.

"She's fine, honey. The doctors want to watch her a little longer to make sure she and the baby are ok. I'm going to take you and Mikey over to Grandma's house tonight, and then your dad will come get you tomorrow morning, ok?" I clipped the last car seat latch and kissed him on the forehead.

Anthony's eyes filled with tears. "I don't get to see my mom today? But I promised her I'd come see her today. She's waiting for me."

"Oh, honey, it's ok. I'm sure she understands you can't come visit every day," I said. Anthony started full-on blubbering.

"Buh... misser." His words came out in shudders.

"Anthony, I can't understand what you're saying. Can you calm down a little and tell me what you said?"

Most of the shudders stopped, and I was able to make out "But I miss her" before globs of snot came out of his nose. I pulled out a Kleenex and wiped his nose off.

I checked my watch. "Ok, I think we have time to go up there really quick and see your mom. Does that sound good?" He nodded.

I was down to about ten minutes of primping time, twenty if traffic was amazingly good. I suppose it didn't really matter. Adam and I had been married for many years, so what was one more evening where I didn't look like I'd stepped off the pages of a magazine. I called my mother-in-law to let her know of the change in plans and to expect us in a little over an hour.

27

I drove to the hospital in Everton and miraculously avoided a speeding ticket.

I shepherded the boys toward Desi's hospital room and paused with them in the hall, just short of her door. I knelt in front of my nephew.

"Anthony, your mom might be resting, so we need to be really quiet, ok? She and the baby need to get as much sleep as possible." Anthony nodded solemnly, his eyes wide.

We tiptoed to Desi's room and peeked in. She lay reclined on the bed with her eyes closed. The TV played at a low volume. Mikey accidentally kicked the curtain divider, causing a rustling noise.

Desi's eyes flew open, and she smiled widely when she saw her son.

"Mommy." Anthony ran to her, tears streaming down his small cheeks. He pressed his head into his mother's side, and she leaned down as far as she could without squishing her massive stomach.

"Thank you," Desi mouthed over Anthony's head. I

nodded. Some things were worth more than looking like a model for my husband.

"I thought I'd bring the boys by to see you before I drop them off at your parents' house," I said brightly, resisting the urge to check my watch again.

"Today's Friday, isn't it?" Desi asked. "Don't you and Adam have a big date tonight? He'd better be taking you somewhere nice. Next time I see that brother of mine, I'm going to remind him how lucky he is to have such a great wife."

I smiled. "I think we're going to the Italian place in downtown Ericksville."

She frowned. "Wow, my brother, the big spender. I always feel like I'm going to see Lady and the Tramp coming out of that place."

"Hey, I like the kitschy décor. And it works perfectly because, as it turns out, the preschool's auction committee meeting is tonight, right down the street from the restaurant."

"Ha! Don't say I didn't warn you about all the 'fun' you'll have with the auction experience." She rolled her eyes. "Nancy's going to wring every drop of energy out of you that she can."

"Hey, I can see a big ship out there," Mikey called from his perch on the windowsill. Anthony ran to him and they both pressed their noses to the glass.

"So how are you doing?" I asked her.

"Ok, I guess," she said. "The latest test results were better, but still not good enough to spring me from this joint. I miss being at home, even the little things like washing dishes or sweeping the floor. Anything to be moving." She looked wistful.

"Well, I've got some great news for you."

Her eyes met mine. "What?"

"Anna Westen told me the sale for the BeansTalk building didn't go through. The café is safe."

Her jaw dropped and then a huge smile swept over her face. "Really? I don't have to worry about it?"

"Really." I hugged her.

"I can't believe it. I've been so worried about the café." Some of the stress lines disappeared from her face. "So how are things with you? How is the job at the condo complex?" She paused. "Oh, I almost forgot to tell you, and you have to promise you won't tell anyone I told you."

I nodded my agreement.

"Tomàs was asking me a lot of questions about Elliott and Perry since he knew I went to high school with them. A few days ago, Tomàs was at the hospital with me and another guy from the force came here to talk with him. Tomàs excused himself from the room, but when he returned, he told me the police found Perry's car at the airport. I bet Perry killed Westen and skipped town!"

"Or he could have been visiting his ex-wife like he said. That's where Elliott said he was going." I tapped my fingers on the bedrail. "But the weird thing is, Perry's ex called the condo sales office and was quite upset that he hadn't arrived yet. You might be right. But why would he kill Westen?" Visions of bribery transactions on a bank statement floated to the forefront of my brain. But it still sounded crazy to me that my neighbor could have taken bribes.

"A few months ago, I attended a town council meeting. Perry was there, petitioning the town council to make an exception to the height restrictions in place downtown," Desi said.

"Height restrictions?" Come to think of it, I hadn't seen any other buildings downtown higher than three stories.

The condo project did stick out like a sore thumb. "Wouldn't that be something they'd have researched prior to construction? What is the height limit?"

"It's limited to three stories. When they started planning the condo project, they were under the understanding that residential buildings were not subject to the height restrictions. But this wasn't something Ericksville had ever had to deal with before. After they broke ground, the town council amended the law to include residential buildings and didn't grandfather anyone in. Perry was so vocal about the unfairness of this after- the-fact change that he made my tantrum look tame in comparison."

"Wow. So did they make an exception?" Was all my hard work on the marketing materials in vain?

Desi shrugged. "I would assume so since they continued building the condos. But think about it—Samuel Westen had a lot of influence on the town council. If he convinced them to go back on their decision to allow the taller building, Perry and Elliott would be ruined." She sighed. "All I know is from the sound of things now, Perry has moved up to the top of the list of suspects in Samuel Westen's murder. Thank God." She took a deep breath, and her eyes filled with tears.

"Jill, I don't think I could have taken much more. It was all so ridiculous. I'm a fat pregnant whale. How do they think I could have drugged a man and then dropped his body off of a cliff? It's insane."

I squirmed a little in my chair. Either Tomàs knew something about the case that I didn't, or he'd lied to his wife about her status with the police. "That's great, Desi."

"What aren't you telling me?" she asked. "You're hiding something." Desi's eyes narrowed. "That policeman wasn't coming here to talk with Tomàs, was he? I'm still a suspect, aren't I?"

"I'm sure Tomàs knows better than I do." I willed myself not to fidget.

"Jill, I know where you keep your chocolate stash. I'll tell Adam, and it won't be safe anymore," she said. "Just tell me the truth."

"Ok, ok." I looked off to the corner of the room. "Yes, as far as I know, you're still a suspect."

Desi crumpled into the pillows and looked out the window for a moment. "What did I do wrong?" she whispered. "First with Ariana, now with this baby. This is all so stupid. I feel like I must have done something wrong to be punished like this."

"Oh, Desi, you didn't do anything wrong." I squeezed her hand. "It's all a big mix-up. And this isn't going to be like with Ariana. The doctors said this baby is doing great. You're doing great. Don't worry about any of the police junk. Nothing matters but the baby."

"They're never going to stop suspecting me until the real murderer is caught." She turned to me. "Jill, you've got to help me. Tomàs can't do anything but what he's been doing because he has to follow police procedures. But you don't have to. You've got to help me figure out who really killed Samuel Westen."

I scanned the room. Anthony and Mikey had moved from the window to the couch, engrossed in whatever show was playing on the TV, and the door to Desi's room was shut. I leaned in.

"I've been checking out some things," I said. Desi looked up at me, hope written across her face. "Something was going on between the Elkins Development Group and Mr.

Westen. I don't know what it is, but I'm going to figure it out."

"Elliott and Perry were always up to something. I can't say I'd be surprised if they were involved with this," she said. "But what was going on?"

"I'm not sure. I have something I want to check up on tonight. I'll let you know what I find out."

I planned to sneak into Mr. Westen's house that night to go through some of his paperwork again. Last time I'd talked to Anna, she'd mention her son having an away game they were traveling to, so I knew she wouldn't be around and I assumed the key to his house was still in its hiding place. I wasn't sure what I was looking for, but something I'd seen previously in his files had caught my eye.

I gave her a quick hug. "Don't worry about it. It sounds like the police are tracking other leads. I'm sure Tomàs is right, and you won't be a suspect much longer." I gave in and looked at my watch. "I'm sorry, but I've got to get the kids to your parents' house if I'm going to get to the auction committee meeting on time."

"Go, go. And thanks for bringing Anthony to see me. I can't wait until I'm out of here." She looked longingly at the door. "I wouldn't want you to be late and incur the wrath of the preschool PTA Queen Bees."

After dropping the kids off at the in-laws, I had about fifteen minutes to get pretty for my date before rushing off to the auction committee meeting. A shower was out of the question, but I had time to curl my hair and throw on a casual little black dress with a fuchsia button-down sweater to wear during the meeting.

~

When I arrived back at the preschool, the parent volunteers were just taking their seats in the back room.

"Jill, over here." Brenda turned in her seat and patted the child-sized chair next to her. I sat down, grateful to see a friendly face.

"Thanks. This has been such a crazy day, and I'd forgotten about this meeting until today."

"I know." Brenda made a face. "I could have sworn this meeting was two weeks away. How's it going with the condo project? Any news for me? I haven't talked with Elliott lately, but I'd love to represent the condos. Do you think you could talk to him for me?"

"I can ask him. You know, it's weird. I asked him about the development of Westen's property, and he said he didn't know anything about it."

She raised her eyebrows. "I'm sure he said it was a done deal. That's really strange."

I shrugged. "I don't know. He's got a lot on his plate. Poor Elliott, he's trying to pick up the pieces of his project, and now it looks like the police suspect his partner in Samuel Westen's murder." I immediately wished I hadn't mentioned the possible connection between Westen and Perry since I'd promised Desi to keep quiet about it.

"Really? I wouldn't have pegged Perry as a murderer. He always seemed like the quiet type, but I guess you can never tell." Brenda shook her head.

"Actually, you're the perfect person to ask. Are you familiar with the zoning laws and height restrictions for downtown Ericksville? Desi told me that, a few months ago, Perry showed up at a town council meeting and was angry about some change in the height restriction law and being told to cease construction on the condos. But they still seem to be building, so I'm confused."

"Oh that." Brenda waved her hand in front of her. "The town council threatened to shut down the project, but what they really wanted was public-use space in the ground floor of the condo. Once Perry and Elliott resolved that issue, the town made an exception for the height of the building. Sounds crazy, but that's how business works in small towns."

Elliott hadn't said anything about public-use space in the building. Was it still a contingency in the condo building plan permits? How formal could that type of deal be?

"Hmm. I'll be sure to include the information about the public space in the promotional materials I'm designing. This hasn't been a very popular project with the rest of the town. If residents know they are getting something out of the deal, it could really help sway public opinion." I sat back in my chair. "Thanks for clearing up my confusion about the height restriction."

Brenda smiled. "No problem. Remember to think of me if Elliott happens to mention needing a real estate agent to help sell units in the building."

Around us, the seats were filling up and parents chatted amongst themselves. I was shocked at the turnout for the auction committee. I'd expected maybe three or four people would get roped into it, but there were at least fifteen people in the small room. I watched as Nancy made her way to the front of the room.

"Ahem." She cleared her throat loudly and beamed at the crowd.

"So nice to see everyone here. I just know this year is going to be such a success," Nancy said. "Let's take a moment to introduce ourselves. As you know, I'm Nancy Davenport, and I've been chairing this event since my oldest child started at Busy Bees Preschool five years ago. Every year I've been involved, we've raised so much money." There was a slight smattering of applause, and Nancy did her best to appear modest.

"Thank you so much. But I did have some help. Although not as much as I'd like," she said in a teasing voice that did little to hide her true feelings.

"And this is Kari Little, our procurement chair. Kari, why don't you tell us a little about yourself."

Kari proceeded to give a three-minute biography and then attention turned to the next person in the circle. My bio was much briefer, but the introductions still managed to eat up a huge chunk of time. I tapped my foot against the chair leg. I didn't want to be late for my dinner date with Adam. It had been too long since we'd spent quality time together.

"Now on to important business. We had scheduled the auction to be held at a venue in Everton, but that has fallen through. Now, we need to find a venue nearby that has an opening in June. Last year Darby Fox's husband, the P.E. teacher at the local elementary school, permitted us to hold it in the school gymnasium, but I think we can do better this year," Nancy said. Darby squirmed uncomfortably in her chair, probably regretting she'd ever heard of Nancy Davenport or Busy Bees Preschool.

"Does anyone have suggestions for a venue? Of course we'd love to keep it local and feel the support of our community, but we also need to keep in mind this is a fundraiser and the purpose is to make money, not spend it."

"How about the Magnuson Cabin at the waterfront park in Everton?" a man in front suggested.

Nancy wrinkled her nose. "That's a great opener, Dan, but let's make some serious suggestions. That place is much too dirty for our auction." The man opened his mouth as if to speak and then closed it, sitting back in his chair and folding his arms across his chest. Nancy had made another enemy. At this rate, I wouldn't be at the top of her list of deadbeat parents.

"Does anyone have a real suggestion?" Nancy asked, eyebrows raised. Chairs squeaked as parents shifted uneasily. No one spoke up.

This would have been a lot more fun if Desi could have attended, but even if she'd been physically able to attend, she wouldn't have touched the auction committee with a ten-foot pole.

I couldn't help but worry about her. Tomàs had succeeded in keeping the police from interviewing his wife again, but he couldn't hold them back forever. Perry was a good distraction for the police, but without concrete evidence against him, the police would be back and Desi would shoot to the top of the suspect list. Still gazing at the floor to avoid eye contact with Nancy, I pulled a small spiral notebook out of my purse and flipped to a clean page. Maybe things would make more sense if I wrote down everything jumbling around in my brain.

<u>Potential Suspects</u>

1. Perry Winston—Seen arguing with Westen at the town council meeting, but issue seems to have been resolved. Supposedly flew to the East Coast for divorce proceedings with his soon to be ex-wife, but she called Elkins Development Group to ask where he was.
2. Anna Westen—Hated her father for selling her mother's land. His death kept him from breaking up the family land even further and allowed her

the chance to save the BeansTalk building from destruction.

3. Desi Torres—Wanted to keep the BeansTalk building from being torn down and losing everything she'd worked so hard for.
4. Elliott Elkins—Did he know he was Westen's grandson?

And then, because if Elliott was a suspect, his mother made an even better suspect:

1. Gwen Hanson—Did she finally get her revenge on Samuel Westen for ruining her life? She had access to the heart medication.
2. Beth Andrews—I'd found her heart medication in Desi's office. What lengths would she go to in protecting her daughter?

None of these people seemed like a murderer to me. Was I forgetting anyone? I tapped the pen against my face. Only then did I realize that everyone in the room was staring at me. What had I missed? My daydreaming had landed me in another predicament. I flushed.

"Jill," Nancy said sweetly, "since you haven't had the opportunity to be very active in the preschool yet, we thought maybe you'd like to propose a location for the auction." Time seemed to stand still and my mind raced. Next to me, Brenda hissed something at me. In my flustered state, I couldn't decipher what she'd said.

"The Boathouse," Brenda whispered a second time.

"The Boathouse," I blurted out. As soon as I said it, the idea made perfect sense. The Boathouse had plenty of space for an auction and dinner, and it was right in downtown Ericksville.

"Too expensive," Nancy said. "We've looked into it before. If you'd attended some of our PTA meetings in the past, you'd know we aren't wealthy. All the profits are invested directly back in the school."

"My in-laws own the Boathouse. I'm sure we can get it at a substantial discount." My words came out faster and faster. "If we held the auction on a weekday, it would be even cheaper. It's a beautiful *and* clean location, and it's less than a mile from the preschool." I started envisioning the table layout and the centerpiece decorations. I could wear an evening gown and look like a million bucks for the first time since before I had kids. When was this auction anyways? I had fifteen Ella pounds left to lose before fitting into my dream dress.

"Well, that settles it," Nancy said. "Thanks, everyone, for coming."

I said goodbye to Brenda and stood to leave.

"Jill, wait." Nancy charged up to me.

"Yes?"

"When can you have a proposal put together for the use of the Boathouse and for your plan for obtaining auction items and attendees?" Nancy asked.

"Excuse me?"

"As auction co-chair, you are responsible for organizing the sub-committees."

"Auction co-chair?"

"Yes, auction co-chair. What we just talked about in the meeting," Nancy said slowly, as though speaking to a child. Apparently my brief moment of fantasy about wearing a beautiful dress had cost me hours of volunteer time.

"Of course. I'll get right on it." I looked at my watch. Five minutes to get over to the Italian restaurant down the street. "Nancy, I'm sorry, but I've got to run."

"Great, I'll help you load the cage into your car."

Cage? My heart sank into the pit of my stomach.

"Lindsey Beecher took the cage outside, but I took the liberty of putting Sugar and Spice into their carrying case," Nancy said, handing me a small pink travel terrarium. Inside the container, the two gerbils huddled inside a toilet paper roll.

I'd been so shocked, I'd taken the object from Nancy automatically, but as we walked toward the door, my hand trembled. I was carrying two squirmy, nasty little rodents. Bile rose up in my throat. Outside, I breathed deeply of the cool air and tried to convince myself that this wasn't an issue, and I wasn't terrified of the tiny creatures. We loaded the larger cage into the back of the minivan, and I placed the gerbils next to their home.

Nancy picked up the travel container and walked around to open my passenger side door. "I think they'll be more comfortable up here with you."

I nodded to her with tight lips. She smiled angelically and shut the door.

Babysitting two rodents was not part of my perfect date night plan. The dashboard clock showed I was a few minutes late for our seven o'clock reservations. I took my phone out of my purse and turned it on to text Adam to let him know I'd be there soon. To my surprise, there were three new text messages on my phone—two from Adam and one from Elliott. I checked Adam's texts first.

"Sorry, honey, our flight got delayed at the Portland airport. Not going to make dinner tonight. I'll see you later." Five minutes later, he wrote, "I'm really sorry. I promise I'll make it up to you. Love you."

Well. That was a perfect end to a perfectly imperfect day. I'd known there was a possibility Adam wouldn't make our date due to his travel schedule, but I'd hoped things would work out this time. I felt like throwing my phone across the front seat. The irrational fear that it would hit the gerbils and cause them to escape stopped me. It was getting pretty chilly out, so I turned on the heater and sat in the preschool parking lot with the car running. I told myself things couldn't get much worse and tomorrow had to be better. I had the start of a new job with Elkins Development Group, two wonderful kids, and a great husband—even if he wasn't around much. With that mantra running through my head, I backed out of the parking space and prepared to turn left to my house. My phone buzzed, and I leaned over to read the text.

"Please let me know if you are coming," read the new message from Elliott. I scrolled up and saw his previous message I hadn't read yet. "We need to get together tonight to go over a new marketing plan. This is big and can't wait until tomorrow."

What could possibly be so big that it couldn't wait until tomorrow? Had Elliott figured out something to persuade the community to support his condo project? What the heck? The kids were at their grandparents' house, and Adam wouldn't be home for hours. What better things did I have to do? A small voice in my head reminded me that this was the way down the rabbit hole in terms of loss of the work/life balance. Still, I texted Elliott back and let him know I'd be there in a few minutes.

28

When I parked in front of the condo project a few minutes later, the sun was setting over Willowby Island. Hues of pink and orange streaked the sky, creating a surreal effect. I grabbed my oversized purse that doubled as a diaper bag and tossed in my cell phone. I pulled my sweater close as a breeze swept through the parking lot.

Before shutting the driver's side door, I looked over at the passenger seat and saw the gerbils in their travel case. With the wind picking up and the sun going down, temperatures would drop quickly. Gerbils had enough fur to withstand cold temperatures, right? One of the creatures smashed its nose against the plastic and stared at me. Mikey would never forgive me if Sugar and Spice froze to death while in my care.

I sighed, pursed my lips, and gingerly picked the terrarium up by its hot pink handle. I didn't want to have to explain to Elliott why I was carrying around gerbils, so I carefully placed the carrier in my purse and wedged it in between a notebook and a packet of baby wipes. The gerbils rustled around in their prison, and I tried to pretend they weren't hanging out a few inches from my waist.

I tried the doorknob of the Elkins Development Group's office, but it was locked. All the lights were off. Where was Elliott? Had he not received my text saying I'd meet him in a few minutes?

"Jill." A man's voice called out from above. Elliott leaned out the open window of a third-story unit. "Up here. The front door is unlocked."

The door was ajar. As I pushed it open the smell of stale smoke assailed my senses. How long would the fire smell permeate the building?

"Elliott?" I called. "Is it safe to go up there?" I looked at the stairs, illuminated only by a thin beam of moonlight. I knew the project wasn't finished yet. They appeared ok, but I was far from being a construction expert. I needed more light. I remembered the laser flashlight attached to my keychain and punched the button at the end of the device. Nothing happened. My cell phone didn't produce much light, but it was all I had. The construction crew had pushed their materials out of the way along the walls, but bits of cement, electrical wires, and blocks of wood were scattered across the concrete floors. I picked my way through the construction rubble to the stairwell and walked up the stairs.

By the third story, I vowed to renew my gym membership. Apparently, pacing my daughter's bedroom for an hour while rocking her to sleep hadn't counted as aerobic activity. I tried to keep the huffing and puffing at a professional level as I walked down the hall to where I'd seen Elliott. Why was he up here anyways?

These units were still under construction and appeared to be untouched by the fire. Without glass in the window frames, the smell of smoke was minimal. Through the west-facing window, the remains of the sunset glowed like the embers of a fire. The effect of the sunset over the water was gorgeous. The future owners of this condo were very lucky people.

"Beautiful, isn't it?" Elliott said, coming up behind me. Startled, I whipped my head around and accidentally hit him with my purse. He stepped uncomfortably close to me, and I sidestepped around him. Where had he come from?

"Yes, very nice. The views are incredible from here. I bet the top floor is unbelievable."

Elliott patted the wide, open window frames. "The panoramic windows will provide the best view in all of Ericksville, maybe even in the North Sound area. These babies are going to go fast when we put them on the market."

"Speaking of listing the condos, do you have a real estate agent in mind for the project?" I asked casually. "Brenda Watkins was just telling me how much she loves this project and would like to be part of it. Especially with the Westen property not being developed, this will be the best view in the area."

Elliott's face grew thoughtful, as though contemplating my question. Then, his face turned scarily pleasant and plastic-looking, the expression reminiscent of that on a Ken doll.

"You know, don't you?" The creepy expression remained on his face.

"Know what?" I had no clue what he was talking about, but the gun he pulled out of his pocket indicated that what he thought I knew was pretty dangerous.

"Don't play coy. I knew you'd figure it out eventually, so I left the stuffed bunny at your house as a warning. You didn't take the hint." He waved the gun at me. "Drop the bag."

My purse fell to the floor, toppling over on its side. My prized faux Gucci sunglasses fell out of the bag and clattered noisily on the concrete floors. Gosh, I hoped they weren't damaged. I needed them to see on the glary gray Ericksville mornings.

What was I thinking? I'd be lucky if I were even alive in the morning, much less able to drive safely. At that moment, it hit me. The black plastic-framed glasses I'd seen Elliott holding at the condo sales office were Perry's. Perry, who by his own admission was blind without them for reading. He never would have left them behind when flying to Baltimore.

I looked up at Elliott. "It was Perry's body they found after the fire, wasn't it? Not some vagrant who'd camped out in the building overnight."

But how was Elliott involved? Why was Perry's car found at the airport? And if Perry hadn't killed Samuel Westen, who had? Things were clicking into place like bricks on a Lego castle.

"Did you have something to do with Samuel Westen's death?"

Elliott's face twisted into something unrecognizable. "That old bastard. He couldn't stand to see someone else in this town succeed in the real estate game. First, it was the height restrictions, and then he came up with some trumped-up regulation about street setback." He waved the gun around. "We'd already poured the foundation. How were we supposed to redesign our entire building on such short notice?"

"So he was blackmailing you to keep the town council

from enforcing the street setback rules?" I edged backward toward the door.

Elliott looked up at me in surprise. "Yes, how did you know?"

"I found the ledger while I was looking for the artist's rendering of the condo project. I knew there was something odd about those payments."

"Ha. Something odd alright. Perry tried to handle it on his own, but I knew something was up when he started drinking again. He'd been sober for two years and then suddenly was hitting the bottle every night," Elliott said. "He finally confessed to me that the money was all gone and Westen still wanted more. That man had the gall to tell Perry he wanted in on the partnership. I wanted to confront Westen, but he wouldn't see me. I had to tell him I was interested in his property. We met in his home office, and that's where I saw it."

While he was distracted by his monologue, I edged further back. My heel caught the edge of a 2x4, causing me to stumble. Elliott saw me.

"Get back over here. I can't let you go now," he said.

I walked back toward him, my mind racing. How was I going to get out of this? What would distract Elliott enough to allow my escape?

"Did you see the photo of your father in his office?"

"Yes." Elliott looked up at me in surprise. "How did you know about my father?"

"I was helping out Samuel Westen's daughter and I saw a photo of your father and mother together. It was the same photo you have on your desk."

"My mother didn't tell me much about my father's family, only that he'd died in an accident during army basic training. When I saw the photo at Westen's house, the pieces fell into place. If it hadn't been for Samuel Westen, my father might not have died, and we wouldn't have had to live like we did. My mother wouldn't have had to work three jobs just to make ends meet." Elliott sounded very tired. "And then he wanted a piece of my business? I'd rather burn the place down than allow that to happen. Once I received the insurance money, I was going to start over somewhere else, but it's taking forever to get the settlement."

"You started the fire? But what about Perry?" The implication hit me. Elliott had killed his best friend.

Elliott's face crumpled. "He was never supposed to be there. Perry should have been on a plane to the East Coast. But because of Samuel Westen, he got drunk and passed out in the demo condo he was living in." Tears pooled in the corners of Elliott's eyes.

"You have to believe me. I'd never have killed Perry on purpose. We'd been best friends since middle school. There isn't anything I wouldn't have done for him, or him for me. That's how he got into this mess in the first place—he wanted to pay Westen off without worrying me, but things went too far. I didn't even suspect Perry was there until the firefighters announced a body had been found in the fire. That afternoon, Perry's soon-to-be ex-wife called to find out why he hadn't made his flight. I saw his reading glasses on his desk and knew he hadn't left. I was enraged. My so-called grandfather had ruined my business and then caused me to kill my best friend. I snapped."

"You killed him to avenge Perry's death?"

"I stopped at my parents' house to bring in the mail the day of the fire and I saw my stepfather's extra heart medication on the counter. Before I knew it, I'd crushed some of his pills and mixed them in with the Scotch I had in the decanter I'd removed from the old condo offices before the fire." Elliott told the tale in a monotonous tone, as though relating someone else's story. "Then I called Westen up and told him I'd decided to buy his property for above market price. He couldn't resist the generous offer. I walked up the hill to his house and brought the Scotch with me to celebrate." Elliott looked up at me and smiled serenely.

"After he drank the Scotch, we walked the property line. When he started feeling dizzy up along the cliff path, I pushed him over the edge. It seemed a fitting end. He'd driven my father to drink, and a drink is what killed him. Afterwards, I walked home and drove Perry's car to the airport. It all worked out so perfectly."

He paused. "Until you started asking questions about developing the property. I was glad I'd hired you to work for me so I could keep a close eye on you. When I went back to Westen's house to look for any evidence linking his son with me, I saw your daughter's rabbit on the floor. I've seen that stupid thing sticking out of your purse so many times, I knew immediately who it belonged to. I broke into your house and left it to warn you off in case you knew something. When my accountant called to say he thought you'd been in my files, I grew even more suspicious. That silly woman, Brenda, was too concerned with money to figure it out and, after you have an unfortunate fall from the third floor of this very building, I won't need to worry about you either."

He motioned to the open window behind him. As if on cue, a breeze came through the window and rustled the paper wrapping on an open bag of construction materials.

I needed to stall him while I figured out an escape plan. "Did you know Samuel Westen paid your college tuition?"

"No." Elliott shook his head. "That's not true. I had a scholarship that paid for everything."

"Westen gave the school that money. I found bank records showing donations made to Willowby College for the four years you were there. I don't think it was a coincidence that you conveniently received a scholarship the same years your grandfather made large donations."

"No," Elliott said again. "He couldn't have. He never knew who I was. My mother had changed her name to my stepfather's last name by the time we moved here, and my stepfather adopted me as well. There was nothing for him to trace to us."

"Your mother was in touch with her family though. Samuel Westen was old and crotchety, but he wasn't dumb. He probably knew about you from the beginning."

Elliott stopped. "It doesn't matter anymore. He's gone and he can't hurt me or my family ever again. Now let's get on with this. The longer we're up here, the greater the possibility someone could see us." He waved the gun and beckoned for me to come closer to the window.

The wind roared through the window again, and some paper near my purse rustled. I dragged my feet along the ground, and Elliott grew more impatient. "Come on, move."

A streak of gray shot across the concrete floor. Before I could react, a second furry creature followed. I screamed and jumped blindly to the side before running toward the highest object in the room, a concrete block near Elliott.

Surprised to see me run toward him at full speed, Elliott backed up. His heels hit the wall behind him and he flung his arms out, the gun clattering to the floor. The panoramic window frame was so wide that he couldn't gain purchase on the walls, and he fell backward through the third floor window. He screamed the whole way down. After a loud thud, there was nothing but silence.

I took the time to search for the rampaging gerbils

before stepping down from my perch, but after a quick glance revealed no twitching tails, I rushed to the window. Below the window, Elliott lay awkwardly on the broken ground. A pool of blood formed below his head and mixed with the mud. I grabbed the cell phone out of my purse and called 911.

29

The police arrived first and the ambulance soon afterward. The twinkling lights on Willowby Island and serene water view were obscured by the flashing emergency lights that lit up the condominium's parking lot.

A police officer I'd never seen before interviewed me near the main door to the condo building. As I watched, the ambulance crew pulled a blanket over Elliott's body, shielding him from the prying eyes of the burgeoning crowd. I shivered and pulled the wool blanket they'd given me closer against my body. My little black dress had turned gray from construction dust, and the thin material was no match for the nighttime temperatures.

"Jill!" A familiar voice called to me from the street. I turned and saw Adam striding across the parking lot. Tears formed in my eyes.

"Sir, you need to stay behind the yellow tape," a police officer said.

Adam pointed at me. "That's my wife. I need to be with her." He ignored the police officer and pushed the crime scene tape aside. When he reached me, he pulled me against his chest. My tears fell freely as the horror of the evening hit me. I had almost died.

"I'm so sorry I missed our dinner date. This is all my fault," Adam said softly in my ear. I snuggled closer.

"How did you know where I was?" I asked.

"Tomàs called me as soon as they told him you were involved. My flight had just arrived at Sea-Tac, and I broke the speed limit the whole way home." His face was etched with worry. I shivered again underneath the blanket, and he wrapped his jacket around my shoulders.

"Officer, is my wife almost done? She's had quite a scare tonight, and I'd like to take her home."

"Yes, just a few more questions." The officer finished his interview and warned me they would need me to come down to the station for more questions the next day.

We walked over to Adam's car, and he helped me into the passenger seat, turning on the heater to warm me up.

"Wait," I said. "My purse. And the gerbils. I left my purse in a unit on the third floor." We both looked up at the window directly above Elliott's body.

He nodded. "I'll ask if I can get your purse." He started to walk away and then turned back to me with his eyebrows raised. "Wait, gerbils? Did you say gerbils?"

"Yes, the gerbils from Mikey's classroom. I had them in their travel container in my purse. When Elliott forced me to drop my purse, the lid on their carrier must have popped open. If it hadn't been for the gerbils escaping and causing a distraction, I may never have gotten away from Elliott." The thought was sobering and, for the first time in my life, I felt something other than revulsion for a rodent. "Can you try to find the two gerbils?" He nodded again, tears in his eyes.

He walked away and conferred with the police standing guard by the yellow tape. Another officer met him at the door to the condo building, and they disappeared inside. Exhausted, I leaned into the heated leather seats and soon fell asleep.

A knocking on my window woke me up. I glanced at the clock and saw that it had been almost an hour. Adam smiled at me and held up both my purse and the gerbils' travel carrier. I had never been so happy to see two rat-like creatures squirming around in a carrier before. He placed the gerbils safely in the back seat and took me home.

30

Four weeks later, the memory of Mr. Westen's murder and the confrontation at the condo building had faded, but I still suffered from flashbacks. However, life moved on, and now our family had something more important to focus on.

I looked down into the cornflower-blue eyes of the newborn baby girl I held in my arms. "Desi, she's beautiful." I snuggled the warm bundle close to me. This was the first time since Lina's birth the week before that I'd been able to hold her as she'd been in the neonatal intensive care unit due to some breathing troubles.

Desi beamed. "We get to take her home in a few days. The doctors think the jaundice will be completely gone by then," she said. "All of those mind-numbing days on bed rest were worth it to have her safely here with us now." Tears shone in the corners of her eyes, and I knew she was remembering Ariana.

I handed Lina back to Desi, and she made a soft cooing sound as she pressed against her mother's curves. I gave Desi a quick hug. "I'm so happy for you and Tomàs. She's perfect. It won't be long until she'll be playing with the other kids." I looked over at Ella. She sat nicely in her stroller, but I knew she itched to practice the inchworm crawl she'd recently learned.

"I told my dad that I want to quit the Boathouse and work full-time at the BeansTalk Café," said Desi.

"Really?" I raised my eyebrows. "How did he take it?"

"He seemed a little disappointed but took it well. It was almost as though he expected it. You didn't happen to mention it to him, did you?" She looked pointedly at me.

I squirmed a little. Somehow she always managed to get things out of me. "I may have mentioned to your mother that you were thinking about making the jump to full-time. But I didn't tell your father, I swear!"

Desi smiled. "You tell my mother anything, you are basically telling my father. She couldn't keep a secret to save her life."

"I'm sorry." My face reddened. "I didn't know."

"Don't be sorry. It takes Dad awhile to get used to an idea, and he's always been so intent on having his kids involved with the business. Adam was always focused on his law career. Neither Will nor Sarah were ever interested in the family business, plus they both ended up living out of the area. I was my dad's last chance, but I think he respects how hard I've worked to make the BeansTalk a success."

"How is everything going with the lease on the BeansTalk?"

"I think it's going to be ok. Anna Westen pushed the town council to designate the building as a historical landmark. While my business will be grandfathered in, the laws will prohibit the building from being torn down or structurally changed. Thank God the property sale Samuel Westen put in motion was never finalized before his death. I hate to say it, but Elliott Elkins did the town of Ericksville a big favor."

Not that I condoned murder, but I had to agree. Samuel Westen had brought misery to everything he touched. I nodded my head. "I'm thankful the property below me isn't going to be subdivided into a million small lots. Anna said she's thinking of renting out the house to tourists. That should be interesting, but not nearly as bad as all that construction and noise from a subdivision."

Ella fussed in her stroller, and I pushed it back and forth a few times before checking my watch.

"Desi, I've got to go. It's almost time to pick up Mikey at preschool. Is Tomàs getting Anthony, or do you want me to get him?"

"No, I'm picking him up tonight. I'm anxious to get things back to normal. Besides, I think this little girl is ready for a nice nap." She walked over to the nurse and let her know she'd be back later.

In Desi's arms, Lina's eyes were closed and her little rosebud lips puffed lightly with every breath. Desi kissed her daughter and gently set her down in her incubator, whispering to her that she'd be back to see her in a few hours. Lina relaxed into the bed, and Desi followed me out of the room.

31

In the parking garage, we parted ways but met up outside the preschool.

"I forgot to ask, how is the auction planning going?" Desi asked, her eyes twinkling.

I groaned. "Thanks for the reminder. Nancy is micro-managing everything. Every day, I regret offering to host the event at the Boathouse. Beth is about to kill me. She says Nancy is even worse than a bridezilla."

Nancy pounced on me as soon I arrived at the preschool. "Jill, just the person I wanted to see. I saw from your latest auction committee report that you plan to use white table-cloths. Doesn't white seem a little passé to you? Blue is popular this year, and I think we should use blue," Nancy said, seemingly in one breath.

I'd explained this to her several times already. "We don't have blue tablecloths in-house. If we want to use blue table-cloths, we'd need to rent them. I thought you wanted to keep on a budget for this?"

"Humph." Nancy said. "What kind of event center doesn't have several colors of tablecloths?"

I counted to ten but was still fuming. In as calm a voice as I could muster, I said, "Nancy, we can talk about this later. Right now, I need to pick up my son. We have some plans that we can't miss."

I pushed past her and Desi followed, leaving Nancy standing alone at the door, her mouth hanging open.

As we waited for our kids to get their backpacks ready to go home, Desi pointed to the table housing the gerbils. "Isn't that a different terrarium than before? I don't remember the castle or the glass structure being so large."

I blushed. "It was a gift from us to the school. In a way, those little buggers saved my life."

"Why, Jill Andrews, don't tell me you like gerbils now," she said innocently. "Pretty soon you're going to be volunteering to take them home every weekend and school break."

I shuddered at the thought. "That's never going to happen."

"As if we would let your family take the gerbils home again. I don't feel like they are safe with the Andrews family after their close call with death last time," Nancy said, coming up behind Desi.

Desi rolled her eyes at me, and I stifled a laugh.

"That's probably a good plan, Nancy." Who knew all I had to do to forever get out of gerbil care was to let them loose in a construction site while someone tried to kill me? It was almost worth it. Almost.

After waving goodbye to Desi and Anthony in the parking lot, the kids and I drove down to the beach.

"We're going to the playground," Mikey said.

"Yes, but we're going to do something else first."

"What?" Mikey asked.

"We're meeting someone here."

"Who are we meeting?" Mikey shielded his face from the sun and gazed across the parking lot.

"Me, silly." Adam grabbed his son from behind and lifted him up to face him. "You and Ella, and Mommy and I are going to have some fish and chips and play on the beach for awhile."

Adam set Mikey back down on the ground, and Mikey bounced around in front of us gleefully. "I want fish and chips! Two pieces of fish, no four pieces, no, one million pieces of fish."

I met Adam's eyes over the kids' heads, and we both grinned.

After wading through the hordes of tourists in line at Elmer's Sea of Fish, we finally got our order and sat down at a picnic table outside the restaurant. Mikey munched away happily on his fish and chips before running off to the nearby playground. Ella alternated between crunching on banana puffs and sucking on fries. The hot summer sun beat down on us, warming away winter's chill.

Adam tipped his head back and smiled. "It seems like weeks since I've seen the sun."

"It has been weeks. Adam, the long hours aren't letting up. You haven't been home before nine for a long time."

"I know, and I wanted to talk with you about it."

"Ok, so let's talk." I hoped it wouldn't turn into an argument and ruin the small amount of family time we had.

"So you know how I've been working long hours to make partner?"

"Yes." I started getting excited. Was he getting close to

making partner? Would the long hours and frequent travel soon be a thing of the past?

"Well, they're talking about making me partner very soon," Adam said. "But I wanted to talk with you first." His face had sobered, and he stared at me solemnly. My heart dropped. Did they want us to move? I'd grown to love Ericksville and our life here.

"What is it?" I was afraid I already knew what he was going to say.

"How would you feel about me going into solo practice? I was thinking about setting up an office in downtown Ericksville. Maybe even in one of the office spaces in the new condo building if they ever get everything worked out with it."

That was most definitely not what I had expected Adam to say. For a minute, I stared off toward where Mikey played on the playground, although I could barely see him through my hazy vision.

"Jill? Did you hear what I said?"

"Yes, sorry." I didn't know what to say. "But you've been working so hard to make partner all these years. And you're so close."

Adam sighed. "I realized that the long hours and frequent travel were never going to end. If I made partner, I'd probably have to work just as many long hours in addition to attending firm social commitments on a regular basis." His gaze turned to Ella and then out to Mikey, who waved at us from the top of the slide. "I'm not sure it's worth it."

My mind churned. How would we afford the loss of Adam's income while he built up clientele? After my near-death experience at the condo building, I'd called Gena to tell her I couldn't take a job that required so many hours and out-of-town travel. My marketing position for the condos had gone out the window with Elliott's death. I mentally assessed our bank accounts and expenses. Our emergency fund should last us for almost a year with no additional income if we cut out the frills. That should give Adam time to get some paying clients. And I could get some kind of job to help out.

I stopped for a moment. Now that Desi had officially told her parents she was quitting, Beth would be all over me to take over her job at the Boathouse. As much as I'd wanted to hate it, I knew it was the perfect job for me. I'd assisted Beth with a wedding the week before and helping to plan and execute the event had been extremely satisfying to me. I knew she'd be eager to watch the kids whenever needed.

"Ok," I said slowly.

"Ok, what?"

"I think you should do it. Open up your own law office." Visions of dinners as a family, shared nighttime feedings, and evenings spent with my husband careened through my mind.

Adam came around the picnic table and held out his hand to me. I stood in front of him, and he pulled me into his embrace for a long kiss.

I knew the future wasn't going to be easy, but this was a step in the right direction, and together we'd taken on any challenges life threw at us. Nothing could be worse than the last two months, right?

FROM THE AUTHOR

Thank you for reading the first book in the Jill Andrews Cozy Mystery series. I've loved writing this series and I hope to write more.

I'm writing a few series at the moment and as a book's success is partially based on reviews, if you'd like me to write more in this series, I'd love it if you'd leave a review on Amazon. Thank you!

Books in this series

Brownie Points for Murder (Book 1)

Death to the Highest Bidder (Book 2)

- coming April 16th, 2018

A Deadly Pair O'Docks (Book 3)

- coming May 15th, 2018

Available on Amazon and Kindle Unlimited

Candle Beach Sweet Romance series

Sweet Beginnings (Book 1)
Sweet Success (Book 2)
Sweet Promises (Book 3)
Sweet Memories (Book 4) - coming April 2018
Available on Amazon and Kindle Unlimited

ACKNOWLEDGMENTS

Cover by: Magic Owl Design

Editing by: Kristen Tate, The Blue Garret

LaVerne Clark Editing

CPSIA information can be obtained
at www.ICGtesting.com
Printed in the USA
BVHW030216210319
543314BV00001B/15/P